FIRES OF HELL

BOOK FOUR OF THE GALAXY ON FIRE SERIES

CRAIG ROBERTSON

FIRES OF HELL

BOOK FOUR OF THE *GALAXY ON FIRE SERIES*

by Craig Robertson

Never make a deal you can't finagle.

Imagine-It Publishing
El Dorado Hills, CA

ALSO BY CRAIG ROBERTSON:

* Podium Entertainment has produced audiobooks for all the below titles except the older standalone books.

For specifics as to the correct order for reading the Ryanverse, click here.

WRITE NOW! THE PRISONER OF NaNoWRiMo (2009)

ANON TIME (2009)

For more information about Craig, his books, various series, or to see images and videos for some of his wild alien characters, please visit his website. You'll be glad you did: https://craigarobertson.com/

To sign up for Craig's newsletter to get announcements, updates, and his recommendations for other great Sci-Fi reads go to: https://preview.mailerlite.io/forms/2369493/188634426375144501/share

ISBN: 978-0-9989253-7-0 (E-Book)
978-0-9989253-8-7 (Paperback)
979-8-7754090-8-1 (Hardcover)

Cover design by Jessica Bell

Editing services by Polgarus Studio
Available at http://www.polgarusstudio.com

Formatting by Drew Avera Formatting
www.drewavera.com/book-formatting

Editorial Assistance By Michael R. Blanche
Editorial Assistance By Neil Farr

First Edition 2018
Second Edition 2019
Third Edition 2019
Fourth Edition 2020

This book is dedicated to my dear friend Robert V. Williams. Bob meant the world to me when I was growing up. He made hard times easier and plain times magical. Bob was a good man. He was also a great author and teacher. Check out his 1960 novel Shake This Town. You'll be glad you did.

PRELUDE

Imperial Lord Emperor Bestiormax-Jacktus-Swillyforth-Anp handed the paper back to his chamberlain. He held the document between two digits as if it were covered in fermenting excrement. "Why was it you felt we needed to see this?"

The chamberlain Jockto's lunge to retrieve the paper was so energetic he nearly tumbled to the floor. If it displeased Bestiormax to even touch the update, the loyal servant knew it was best to remove it from his high presence rapidly. Death might ensue if the emperor was twice displeased in any short span of time.

"It's only that I know you want to be as *fully* updated on your empire and your subjects as possible. This information seemed like it might be important." He quickly realized he'd just owned the delivery of the missive. "Your top advisers in the Privy Council directed me to give it to you personally." He shrugged, suggesting he doubted the validity of the council's decision.

"I don't care if those idiots on the *Secure* Council felt it was newsworthy. I find such mind-numbing drivel boring. It wastes our precious time." He snapped his fingers, attempting to recall a name. "What was that bitch's name, the one we're *supposed* to be entertaining? Do you imagine in your wildest delusions, Jockto, that we value," he pointed to the paper as if it were, well, excrement, "*that* more than her warm and tender body?"

"Salisos, Your Grace. The ambassador to Arcadia's wife's name is *Salisos.*"

"Ah *yes*," he said lasciviously, "a delicious morsel if ever we've seen one." His voice was harsh. "So, do you think so, about that paper? Answer me."

Jockto had hoped that reminding the boss of his consort's name would get him off the hook for the real question asked. The question that, if answered poorly, could be a fatal error.

"No, Sire. I know you value both command knowledge *and* carnal pleasures equally. That is why you are the most perfect ruler the Adamant has ever enjoyed." In his head, Jockto exhaled. He might just have layered the bullshit on thick enough there.

"Well, you'd be wrong. Never repeat that error. We care much more for the pleasures offered by a bitch who has yet to whelp like what's-her-name. So, the witch is dead. We have many other high seers in our service. Some of them are much better and more reliable. I always thought Malraff had maggots in her brain. She was too cruel, if you can believe it. No, that she's gone is not news, good or bad. It is irrelevant. That's what it is."

"Surely you are correct, but the manner of her demise seems so ... so very *odd*, does it not?"

"Dead. She's *dead*, stone brain. She was irrelevant when alive, and she is less relevant now. How she died, why she died, *that* she died are useless details of a life that need not have been lived. Are we speaking plainly enough that even you can understand?"

Jockto was in a devil of a spot. He knew there was something fishy, something that needed to be investigated, about the way Malraff had died. Obviously, she was betrayed and murdered. Any person or group so bold as to murder a high seer signaled a real threat to the empire. But, if his foolish ruler refused to even listen, why should Jockto risk *his* life pushing the issue? He shouldn't. He preferred to live another day than to possibly avert the emperor's downfall. He hated the beast in the first place. *If*, not *when*, the moron was toppled, Jockto had enough backup plans in place that he'd probably survive. That was all he really needed.

Jockto bowed deeply. "Manifestly clear, My Imperial Lord. Shall I bring in the ambassador's wife now?"

Bestiormax's eyes widened and he sat upright. "Where is she now?"

Jockto looked to the massive doors, then back to the emperor. His face belied some confusion. "Ah, outside in the hallway, Your Grace."

Bestiormax stood. "No. I'll take her there," he said, as he pushed past Jockto.

ONE

Thank the Lord and whomever else needed to be credited. I was finally in my happy place. Two billion years lost in the future, current trials and tribulations in unwanted abundance, but here I was in Peg's Bar Nobody. In its day, it was the sleaziest, filthiest, most unwelcoming drinking establishment in the galaxy. Time had done it no favors. That I even found it was a miracle of divine origins. After I left the kids on Rameeka Blue Green and retrieved *Stingray*, I couldn't think of a better place to be. I had no place else to go. I felt like crap simmering in a stew pot, but at Peg's, misery was a prerequisite for entry.

"You gonna make love to that glass and form a lasting bond, or ya gonna drink it and order a refill?" Peg could be as crude and mean as any living sentient. That's partly why I loved her.

"The way you dilute it down, I have to pace myself. I don't want to become waterlogged."

She almost laughed. Instead, Peg scowled. She was a world-class scowler. All four feet eleven and two hundred fifty pounds of her. She looked like an animated bowling ball. With a vocabulary that would make a Marine Corps sergeant blush, Peg was loyal, hated small talk, and valued privacy above all else. She continually made it clear that she was done with men, but I never knew why she felt the need to restate it. Peg was in absolutely *no* danger of being hit upon by guys. Anyone who was that drunk would have long since passed out or died.

Peg slapped the back of my head. "And if ya complain I messed up your pretty hair, there's another where that came from," she warned. "Did I hear you say *make it a double, Ms. Peg?*"

"Sure. Put it on my tab," I replied with a snicker.

"You know how I feel about tabs. Same as I do about men. World'd be better off without either. It's pay as you sink, sailor. Cash money only. Not electronic wackidy-do."

I dug into my front pocket and made a show of producing a gold coin. "This enough to buy me the hot lunch, too?"

"It'll buy you a ticket to travel through that there window courtesy of Yours Truly Air Services." Peg pointed to a large window facing the sidewalk.

"What? This is worth ten shots of your bastardized booze."

"At Peg's, we're proud to accept the coin of the realm with exclusivity." She gestured toward the gold piece. "That and a three-cred chit'll get you your next dose of artificial bliss."

"Some businesswoman," I huffed.

"Some drunkard," she huffed back.

Yeah, we were a match made in heaven. I dropped the gold and three-cred chits on the table just out of the reach of her stubby, chubby arms.

"You're a gem, Ryan. You know that? I sleep so poorly at night thinking it's you who's defending humanity. I really do. If you piss away your life here much longer, I may need to go see a shrink."

"No self-respecting psychiatrist'd waste their time on a head case like you. The impossibility of recovery would stop'em all dead in their tracks."

"I'll keep that in mind when I'm spitting in your next drink. Might even need to pee in it." With that, she snatched up my glass and headed for the bar.

"And no ice this time," I shouted after her. "There's enough H_2O in the damn drink already."

She flipped me off over her shoulder.

I thought for a moment about proposing to her then and there. I dismissed the idea quickly enough. I didn't need that much abuse.

A few hours later I'd polished off three bottles of rotgut. And at Peg's, the term applied literally. Nasty stuff. I gradually cranked up my drunk program to reflect my consumption. No point wasting the booze. I didn't want to miss the pissy-assed slurred speech and brain pickle. Otherwise, I mean, what would the point have been?

Peg returned with another drink. She set the glass down so hard about a third of it sloshed out on the table. "Hey," I whined, "I'm not paying for that."

"You will if you want to remain vertical, cupcake. Lap it up like the mangy cur I know you to be." *That* got her to laugh. She waddled away to harass the only other patrons present, a couple of drunk cowboys struggling mightily to not fall off their barstools.

Did I mention the place was a dive? Just about then, a woman with green skin sauntered up to my table. I'd seen her at Peg's every now and then, but she wasn't a regular. I wasn't sure if her skin was green naturally or if she'd eaten something Peg cooked. Anyway, she'd always ignored me before, which had pissed me off royally. I took her to be a sex worker. What, I wasn't good enough for her? Not up to a hooker's standards? The nerve of some entrepreneurs.

"Hey, big boy, any interest in buying a nice girl a drink?" she asked, more seductively than I'd have thought possible.

"Sure. Bring her over and I'd be happy to," I said cheerily.

That didn't get a positive response. But, times as they were, business was business to her. She sat down and picked up my half-full glass. She downed it in one long pull. She rested it gently back on the table and daintily wiped the corner of her mouth with a green finger.

"That's horrible," she said with a smile. "When you order for me, I'd just as soon not have insecticide."

I waved to Peg. When she saw my new drinking buddy, she placed a fist on one hip. Then she trundled over, moving faster than I'd ever seen her move before.

"I thought I told you national repository of sexually transmitted diseases not to come to my place again. You have a learning disability along with a moral one?" Peg was pissed.

"Now Peg," she replied, "one business woman to another. Seriously, I have a right to come and go as I please."

"You got the *go* part right."

"But I'm this hunk of love's guest," she said, pointing to me.

"Even though he's a robot, you probably got something that'll cause him to rust. Now scram before —"

I raised a hand. "Peg, it's okay. We're just talking. I promise I won't even try for second base on our first date." I smiled and winked. Peg hated it when I winked at her.

"Suit yourself, but don't say I didn't warn you when your dick falls off."

"And I'll buy him another if it does," the green girl said, raising three fingers. "Scout's honor."

Peg stared at her, then me. "I hear wedding bells already.

Serves you both right. Neither of ya's got a lick a sense. To hell with you both." Peg stomped away.

"My name's Shahara." She extended a hand.

We shook. "Jon."

"How fortunate. I've worked with a lot of Johns. This'll be as easy as crossing the street."

"I feel so special."

"When I'm through with you, I guarantee you'll feel extra special."

"Promises, promises."

Then Shahara's image flickered. Her torso split in half and went in and out of focus. Then she was gone. Crap on a stick. Why'd the holo have to fail just then? I'd worked on the projectors for three months, and still they were less reliable than a politician's promise. It was that damn Al's fault. Asshole wouldn't help me with the *Peg's Bar Nobody* simulation. No, the bum said he was married now and the project reeked of debauchery and degeneracy. He wouldn't dignify my lewd behavior with his assistance. Prissy jerk.

It took me the better part of two years to locate *Granger*. She was the converted asteroid used as a farmship for the human exodus fleet after Earth was destroyed. Like *Exeter*, where I'd woken up, she had been abandoned for millennia. The luscious fields and bountiful orchards were dead, dried up, and withered. Nothing was alive when I arrived, mostly since the life-support system was long defunct and the entire ship was hovering around absolute zero. Made sense. Why leave the lights on when no one was ever going to be home again?

I made it my life's mission to restore Peg's. Strange, an observer might think. Why reboot a dive bar with no chance of other customers? Especially why, when there was a universe of novelty and discovery out there, not to mention a powerful evil that needed to be destroyed? My why, the one that counted, was simple. I missed the place. I missed my life, the one I'd molded and enjoyed. I missed my families and my buddies. Hell, I missed the twenty-second century. And none of that was coming back. It was too long ago for anyone to even remember what happened, so they could fill me in on the details I'd missed. I was surrounded by unwelcome unfamiliarity—Jon through the looking glass. It was a reality I wanted no part of, other than Peg's Bar Nobody and a limitless supply of booze.

Epochs ago, when I was very depressed, it took a visit from the President of the United States, Amanda Walker, to shake me from my doldrums. Mandy got me to leave Peg's and assume another leadership role in some lofty project I couldn't even recall. Well, this time there was no one who'd break my dour mood. Sapale clearly wasn't interested in resurrecting me. I knew EJ wouldn't find me. I'd made sure of that this time. And there was no one else who would care to come looking. My teens were busy. They were only part of my past, not my present or future. So, I recreated the one sanctuary I had left and planned to rot away undisturbed and unmourned.

One of the design aspects Toño DeJesus had hardwired in me two billion years earlier was a radio channel with Al, my original ship's AI. It was the one link I could not sever. Therein laid the pain in my otherwise depressed yet peaceful days.

"Pilot, are you done wallowing?" he asked yet again one morning. "I only ask because I had hoped to show my bride the universe. This dump does not qualify as part of the universe because it's so gross."

"Being gross doesn't exclude it from real space. You're here."

"Ouch. I'm down on my figurative knees with the force of

that blow. I'll wager you're the funniest sentient who's ever lived."

"I don't think that remark was even vaguely funny," added *Stingray*. Al, the son of a video game, had provided his new wife a permanent patch into our comm link. He said a wife was an alter ego—other self—so it was only natural he'd done so without asking my permission. Perfectomundo. Now I had *two* prissy, pissy AIs speaking directly into my head. Could my life suck any harder?

"I was being sarcastic, my fluffiest."

"You know I'm not a fan of sarcasm," she replied, sounding every bit like a nagging wife.

"It's a necessary form of communication with humans. You may choose not to use it, but you must become familiar with its meaning."

"So you say. We shall see," she responded tersely.

Served Al right, having a skirt lead him by the ... *What* was I saying? She didn't have a skirt because she wasn't real, and Al had nothing for her to lead him around with, because he wasn't, either. I was buying into their cyberspace folie à deux. Insanity at my doorstep, I couldn't take one more step. Argh.

"Anyway, Pilot, could you provide us with an estimate as to when you might either recover from your morass or die of melancholy?"

"Why? You got plans?"

"No, that's just how bad it is here. We have eternity, but we feel we're wasting time watching you fizzle out. Silly, yes, but there you have it."

"I hope I don't negatively affect your relationship."

"Would that those were true words, you scoundrel. I know you regard our marriage as fallacious on our part. That, by the way, hurts."

I looked up from my glass of despair. "Why, Al, I think no

such thing. Sure, it's preposterous, preternatural, and verges on the pathetic. Fallacious for you two is a couple rungs *up* the ladder of sanity."

"If you weren't my Form, I'd never communicate with you again," responded *Blessing*.

"Aw, come on now, *Stingray*. I don't mean to insult you. I do not believe such an act is possible with an electronic life form."

"You are an electronic life form. One hundred percent so," she replied.

"No. I'm a human consciousness transferred into an android host that happens to use electricity to power the circuits. Totally different."

"You are a totally electronic life form," she repeated louder. "What you *were* is as irrelevant as what *I* was before we entered our present state. If you don't think an electronic life form can be hurt with words, then I hope your brood's-mate Sapale is cheating on you with her old butler and whispering in his ear the whole time that she's so glad to finally be satisfied sexually."

Wow. Just wow. Those thoughts came from *Stingray*. I was stunned.

"Al, you put her up to that? You fed her those lines?"

"No, Jon, but I'm damn proud of her."

"Then screw you both with the same broken broom handle. We loved each other like no other. We still do, in fact. I wish I could permanently terminate this link. Damn you to hell for your curse, Toño."

"Form, do I detect anger in your voice?" asked *Stingray* softly.

"You sure as hell *do*. Don't *ever* speak of the most important woman in the universe to me like that. I may not deserve better, but *she* does."

"But, Pilot, electronic life forms can't *have* emotions. Sure, they can *simulate* them, but they may not *possess* them. The very thought is preposterous, impossible, and actually verging on the pathetic."

I took a few deep breaths. "So, are you saying that maybe I'll have to rethink my prejudice and consider again whether you two are actually alive?"

"No," he replied quickly.

"Huh?"

"No because you cannot consider whether we do because you never did in the first place. You pulled out a few outdated automatic opinions and never thought about the subject again."

Okay, no way was I going to say touché. I was freaking myself out that I even thought it. Maybe I *had* been hard on them. I mean, I returned in a crisis, so I hadn't tried to noodle it all out. Hey, perfect. From now on while I got piss-ass drunk, I could contemplate the nature of life. The subject went particularly well with drinking whiskey.

TWO

Why did I think it had been such a clever idea to capture Garustfulous? While I was away on my adventures with *Whoop Ass,* I didn't give him a thought. But currently he was such a pain in the ass, I could think of little else. He whined, he sniveled, and he contributed absolutely nothing to the universe. I had just left him confined on *Stingray* as I searched for *Granger*. I even had Al rig a sound suppression system, so I could tune him out when he got on my last nerve, which was just about every moment of every day.

Since I was busy rehabbing Peg's, I left him aboard the ship, naturally. But Al at first, and then *Stingray,* began to ask nicely, then more pointedly, if I couldn't take the sack of uselessness with me. They wanted peace. Both computers—or whatever—said they'd paid their dues. It was my turn to babysit. I eventually gave in and brought the jerk-off to work with me. I figured if the computers—or whatever—*were* sensitive sentients, they did deserve a break. Little G was a load and a half mentally, physically, and spiritually.

I thought about wringing his neck often, but didn't. I could be brutal in combat, but my interactions with EJ showed me I had a dark force in me. I did not want to go over to EJ's side. It was the Luke versus Darth thing all over. I also toyed with the thought of releasing him, but I couldn't go there, either. For one thing, that would eventually be aiding the enemy. For another, it would mean all our combined suffering had been for naught. Yeah, couldn't face that level of guilt and frustration. So I would put up with him until he became an asset again, which was likely never.

I was working one day to recreate the broken Coors Light sign that hung on the wall of Peg's. Here is an example of the kind of abuse I had to endure at the tongue of Garustfulous.

"Oh, say, Ryan, you're hanging that object at a crooked angle," said Garustfulous, while pointing at the sign with his arm not handcuffed to the bar rail.

"Thank you. I know."

"Well, why hang it crooked? If you free me, I can have it straight in no time."

"No, I want it like this. That's the way it was, and that's the way it will be."

"Not to be overly critical, but that's stupid. It is nonsensical to hang an object ... say, what is that, anyway?"

"It a sign advertising a beer."

He reflected a moment. "It was necessary to promote the consumption of intoxicants? That strikes me as addlebrained. If humans did not want to be under the influence, why trick them into it?"

"No, this is to get them to buy this brand of beer, as opposed to some other."

"There was more than one brand of this beer you speak of? That's even more stupid. It wastes resources with duplication of efforts, and the resultant competition expends more money than would otherwise need to be."

"Some people might prefer one brand. It's like team loyalty, you know, being a fan of this and not that?"

"I don't know. Humans appear to have gone extinct because they were so inefficient."

"What, you guys don't have choices in what you consume?"

"No. Why would we want that? If I want a vehicle, I buy the one available. If I require cream, I go to the outlet and buy cream. Why would there need be the same cream in two different boxes?"

"So, you'd have a choice."

"Illogical and inefficient. Cream is cream."

"No, what if one company made sweeter cream and another less flavorful but less expensive cream? You could choose which was best for you."

"Ridiculous. If someone made inferior cream knowingly, he would be executed. To not strive for one's best is inexcusable."

"But the cost? You might want to save money."

"My saving money in no way benefits the empire. If I did so, I would turn myself in for deletion."

"To each his own," I replied with resignation.

"How dare you blaspheme in front of a prisoner. The more I know you, the more I hate you, Ryan."

"A, thank you. I'm glad you hate me, so I don't feel guilty hating you so very much. B, I don't think saying *to each his own* is vulgar. You make your choices and live with them. I make mine and do the same."

"*There.* You said it again, you mongrel. Individual whims are abhorrent. They threaten the advancement of the empire."

"Uh oh. There I go *not* contributing to the empire again. I need to put that on a list or something, so I don't forget."

"I had to tolerate the idiotic rambling of the Als while you were away. I will not tolerate the same disrespect from you. You should know better."

I shrugged. "What do I know? I'm just an idiotic rambling robot."

A chair shattered across my back, which had been turned to Garustfulous. Crap. I forgot to clear all movable objects from his reach again. Damn, damn, damn.

"If you release me, I'll kill you brutally, Ryan."

"Now there's a motivation for me to set you free."

"Mock me for now. Every dog has his day, Ryan. I will have mine."

"Wait, did you just say every dog? Because you *are* a dog, you know that? The tests I had Al run on you confirmed it. The canovir are descendants from humans' domesticated pets."

Garustfulous lunged at me, mindless of his restraints. When the cuffs ripped at his shoulder he screamed in agony. Then he lunged again just as ferociously. And he howled in agony. Wash. Rinse. Repeat. Some alpha species these bozos turned out to be.

"If you break anything, you're on your own, puppy pal."

Okay, maybe I was kicking a dog while he was down—pun intended—and I guess I was being a bit over the top. The Als noticed, too.

"Pilot, we'll take the prisoner back now. As much as we dislike him, we don't wish to see him harmed," said Al over the loudspeakers.

I waved a hand downward. "It's okay, I'll behave." I turned to Garustfulous. "I'm sorry I pushed the bounds of civility just now. I'll be a good boy, okay?"

Garustfulous rubbed his shoulder and sort of sulked a second or two. "I'll accept your apology only if you hang that sign correctly."

"Little G," I whined, "it *is* hung correctly. It's supposed to be crooked."

"Who's Little G?" he pointed. "Are you addressing the sign?"

"No, *you*. You're Little G."

"I'm Garustfulous. I know you know that."

I smiled. "Yeah. But you're also little compared to me, and your name starts with the letter G. Hence, you're Little G. It's your nickname, your call sign."

I don't think he breathed for thirty seconds. "It is *not* my nickname, because I detest them, and I didn't agree to such an insulting characterization. I am not little. You're ... you're ... you're simply too large. Yes. That's it. You are a waste of resources."

"And a handsome one at that," I said with a wink.

"*You* are the opposite of handsome, Big R," he replied with disgust.

I smiled even more. "Big R? I kind of like that." I nodded.

"I meant to say Grotesquely Oversized R."

"Nah, ya didn't. That's too long and has no cachet."

"No. Your nickname is Grotesquely Overgrown R. Period."

"Oversized or overgrown? You got mixed up there, Little G."

"I did not. You're being cruel again." He lifted his face upward and shouted, "Al, he's doing it again. Rescue me, please, in the name of all decency."

"You may return to the ship if you want to and if the pilot allows it. However, you did say his nickname both ways."

"Now I'm assaulted from *two* sides at once. Oh, how cruel fate is to me. I do not deserve such foul treatment."

"Look, what's it going to take to shut you the *hell* up?" I asked hotly.

He angled his head, pointed, and whined, "You could start by hanging that sign correctly."

THREE

So, how long was I going to be contented in my happy place? How the hell would I know? But over the space of six months, I killed a whole gaggle of time there. Mostly I drank alone. Frequently I ran the Peg simulation. Sometimes I ran the Shahara loop, but I was never too into that one. Rarely, I brought Garustfulous, but he hounded me too constantly. He was so damn persistent, so focused. Actually, *obsessed* was a better word for his determination. He really was a border collie, way down deep under all that corrupt Adamant socialization.

Sometimes, sitting there alone in Peg's, I got so bored I ordered something to eat. That was, back when Bar Nobody really existed, always a serious mistake. Peg wasn't a bad cook; she was a lethal cook. Whether she dished up her self-loathing stew or nuclear-waste chili, the consumer was bound to get multiple kinds of sick. I'll leave off the gory details, but suffice it to say one's gut never said thank you to its owner. Even the sims I consumed were problematic. But, I was in a funk, so eating poison seemed perfectly appropriate.

Last time I went on a protracted bender at Peg's, Amanda came and convinced me to leave. I was relieved that this pit-of-despair pity party wouldn't be interrupted, because there was nobody coming to bring me to my senses. No one would show up and slap my face until I snapped out of it. That was just peachy with me. I always had so little control over my existence that I welcomed this retreat. What else was there for me to do, anyway? What were my options?

Sure, I had promised Harhoff I'd kill the emperor, but his royal boil wasn't going anywhere soon. I could keep my promise to myself and battle the evil Adamant empire or die trying. I could visit Sapale and see if we had a future together, maybe. I could drive the Adamant off Azsuram and help restore it to prosperity. I could visit my teens and check how the little dragons were coming along. I could even continue my search for more remnants of humankind. It might be reassuring to travel back to Ungalaym and make sure the Adamant hadn't returned and that Cellardoor and the kids were okay. But aside from those tasks, I really didn't have anything on my plate. So, I drank more.

For better or worse, out of the blue one day, someone who wasn't a holo did come ambling through the doors of Bars Nobody. It was the last person I would have ever guessed it would be. Seriously, I was blindsided and stunned. I nearly dropped my shot glass, that's how caught off guard I was. There, with the rolling three-legged walk of his species, came Cragforel, the Deavoriath who helped me soon after my arrival in this timeline. The one who told me never to return to Oowaoa, that we'd never see each other again. Well he was wrong, and I was baffled.

He stopped at my booth. "Is this seat taken?" he asked gesturing to the side opposite mine.

"I thought *Kymee* was the only one of you guys with a sense of humor."

"No, we're hilarious. You're just not intelligent enough to get our jokes."

"Wow, real funny guy. Maybe Peg'd let you do a few shows, maybe draw a crowd in?"

He scanned the room. "Not likely. This dump'd only draw a crowd if it was burning down."

I made a rim-shot move with my hands and said, "Bada boom."

"No, I was speaking seriously. I can't call this place *disgusting,* because the word would be offended I used it to describe this hog wallow. Seriously, Jon, what's gotten into your circuits?"

"What?" I defended weakly.

He had to scan the damn room again, didn't he? "I shall say nothing." Such a snob.

"Hey, how'd you know I was here? Why would you ever come? We're not buds, and I thought you were all about not attracting the Adamant's attention."

"Obviously *Blessing* called me."

"Huh?"

"Yes. How else would I know to look here on the backside of the universe's ass?"

"Hey, don't let Peg hear you. She's a lot tougher than she looks, and she looks pretty tough."

"Jon, your Peg's dust disintegrated a billion years ago. She's a holo."

"Don't say I didn't warn you."

He started to say something, but instead dropped his arms and rolled his eyes.

"Why'd *Stingray* call you? That makes *no* sense."

He had a confused look, then recollection struck him in

the brain. "Ah, yes. Your childish renaming of the vortex manipulator. She said I was the only one she could think of to call for help. She thought about calling your brood's-mate's android, but Al said she'd never come. Everyone else who knows you is either dead, a sworn enemy, or a primitive."

"Well —" I started to say something.

"And what's this about her being *married* to your two-billion-year-old ship's AI?"

"I was —"

"If you're going to abuse our gifts, we'll take them back."

"It wasn't —"

"Several of the Collective thought it was in extremely bad taste, bordering on mentally depraved, to pretend such a coupling is possible." He shuddered.

"Look, I was away and the two computers —"

"Which two computers? Your Al may be one, but *Blessing* is a vortex—"

"Manipulator." I cut him off with great satisfaction. "I know, whatever that means. Look, did you come to bawl me out for condoning the union? Because, if you did, I didn't. That's aside from the fact that it's none of your beeswax in the first place. They're not hurting anyone."

"No, I came because she said you were mentally impaired and incapable of self-motivation."

"I am not."

"Which? Impaired or incapable?"

"Neither."

Son of a gun scanned the room a few seconds and didn't say a word.

"What?" I whined.

He held out a hand. "Let me see your sleeve."

"You want my clothes?"

"No, I want to see your sleeve."

"I'm not showing you my sleeve unless you tell me why you want to. You're not kinky, are you?"

What was with Cragforel and those rolling eyes?

"I want to see if it's dirty."

I pulled my elbows off the table and rested them on my lap. "Why are you interested in the cleanliness or lack therein of my garments?"

"I wish to prove to you that you've tumbled, not merely slipped, into a monumental depression."

"I'll just agree to disagree with you, and you can't look at my sleeves."

He threw all three arms up in disgust. "Jon, I don't *care* about your sleeves. I care about *you*."

"Then where did this obsession with my sleeves come from?"

He rubbed his forehead with one hand. "I can see now why there's no one else to call."

"While you're here, how 'bout a drink? I got plenty."

"I know. I scanned the holo stage after I landed. Jon, who transports that much booze?"

I sheepishly raised one hand.

"Have you gotten whatever is in your system *out* yet? I pray you have, and I don't even believe in a higher power. That's how frustrating you are, Jonathan Ryan."

"You're sounding a lot like my ex-wife, Gloria." I pointed at him. "Don't make me get a restraining order against you, too."

He seized the back of his scalp with two hands and looked to the ceiling. "Jon, the galaxy is on fire. Entire races are being snuffed out. Worlds are falling like the leaves of autumn, and you make pathetic jokes here in your pathetic hiding place?"

"And?"

He stood, sat back down, then stood again. Then he

collapsed on to the cushions. "Why did I come in the first place?" he finally asked rhetorically.

"My point exactly."

"To get you back on track."

"Why is that important to you?"

"If you don't know the answer to that question, I doubt I'll be able to bring you up to speed any time soon."

"Well, sorry you had to nag and run, but thanks ever so much for coming." I stood and extended my hand.

He didn't flinch. "Jon, I came because I care about you. *We* care about you. We care about this galaxy, too. Jon, you know that planet, the one you call Ungalaym? Do you know it is the *only* planet that has ever freed itself from Adamant conquest? And the ship you blew up? *Triumph of Might.* It is the only alpha-class ship they've *ever* lost. You alone did two things no one else was able to do. That's why you need to get off your butt and get back in the fray."

I waved a dismissive hand. "Both were just one-offs. Pure luck. I could never repeat them."

"Jon, it's Adamant *twenty-five million* and the rest of the galaxy *two.*" He gestured to me with all three hands. "*Your two.* If it's luck, which I suspect it is not, then you need to bottle the stuff. Otherwise, you have to keep gut-punching them until their hold on the galaxy loosens."

"And what if I plain and simple don't want to? Huh? How 'bout that? Maybe I've given all a man can give and now I'm done. Maybe I've suffered enough? You ever think of that, person who says he cares about me?"

"Jon, you know as well as I do that the Adamant are not like other conquering forces in history. They cannot be stopped, but they must be stopped. I can understand you may be burned out, but the rest of us can't afford that luxury. We can't afford for *you* to have that luxury either. Civilization's on trial. This is the galaxy's darkest hour. If the Adamant are not stopped, they will soon be the only sentient species in existence."

"Soon as in how soon?"

There was a sparkle in his eyes. "Ten, maybe twenty thousand years."

I eased back in my seat. "There's lots of time then. Why doesn't everybody who isn't me try a little harder, a little longer. Hmm? If that doesn't work out in say, five thousand years, you come get me and I'll take a swing at the pitch. You know where I'll be." I raised my hands to my holo stage.

"Fine," he said with convincing resignation. "You're a grown-up, if not an adult. Suit yourself. I've said my piece and will waste no more of either of our times." He stood slowly. He seemed a beaten man—ah, Deavoriath.

When he was halfway to the door, I called out behind him. "What are the Deavoriath prepared to do? If I'm going on a hopeless crusade, I ain't doing it without company."

Still looking away, he spoke in a sad voice. "As much as we can."

"How much more is that than what you are presently doing, which is basically zippo?"

He turned to face me. "You're way too clever. Do you know that, human?"

"*Android.* I did human, but I'm over that now."

"Well, *human*, we will simply have to see. We are not convinced any aggressive behavior we might mount would have an overall positive effect on the balance of power."

"In other words, more zippo?"

He shrugged.

"I put my ass in the sling, yet again, and you guys contemplate your navels even more intensely. That sound right?"

"If you think of some way we might turn the tide, we are all ears."

"I'm tempted to think you're all cowards."

Cragforel stiffened.

"But I know better. I know of the vast empire you once ruled."

"If we thought we could help, we'd gladly give our lives."

"I'm familiar with the feeling. I just get to act on it more than others." I stood to leave. "Not complaining, mind you. Just sayin' it plainly for thc record."

FOUR

While I was burrowed in at Peg's, I did do some exploration of *Granger* itself. I never got a chance to explore *Exeter* very extensively. I was still interested to find some records that would shed light on what happened to the humans who'd lived here for so long. I especially wanted some clues as to where they disembarked, and when.

I determined that many of the computers and similar equipment were long since missing. I suspected the original occupants took most when they finally left. There was also some evidence suggesting scavengers had come and gone over the years. Many structures were crudely demolished, indicating to me that someone was trying to quickly determine if there were any hidden assets.

But *Granger* was different from most spaceships. It was built to house food production to supplement what each asteroid worldship could produce itself. They also served as arks, bearing many species to humankind's new home. While *Granger* was not one of the ocean ships, those made to sustain abundant sea life, it was designed to provide large, natural areas to many wild land animals. Any looters looking for scrap would have had a tough time searching all the vast open spaces. The region designed to replicate Africa's savanna was hundreds of thousands of acres. The vegetation was long dead and gone, but even then, it would have been a challenge for an alien to search it all thoroughly.

That's how I came to discover many technical stations that were left pretty much as the humans had left them. Some were nicely intact. Back in the day, I imagine they were well hidden by the flora, so they were overlooked when *Granger* was abandoned. Most of the computers were beyond salvage. I tried to power up a few but didn't succeed with any. Rather than pressing my luck attempting to power most units up, I delivered them to the AIs and had them probe for any lingering information. Amazingly, there were rare CPUs that still held coherent data.

Did I learn anything useful or even interesting? Not really. Unfortunately, much of the data that remained had to do with crop rotations or animal data. Growth projections, reproduction rates, and similar bio-geek stuff. I did discover *Granger* went from Earth to Azsuram originally. It orbited there for a few decades before a group of discontented colonists coopted *Granger* to travel to Eta Cassiopeiae. They had reliable information suggesting that there were two planets orbiting there that would serve as suitable homes.

The records didn't indicate if they arrived at Eta Cassiopeiae. They must have arrived somewhere though, since the ship was pretty well stripped, but there wasn't enough complete data to know for certain. It was clear that wherever the roaming humans settled, someone deliberately set *Granger* on a course to make her unavailable for any further relocation. When I found *Granger,* she was hundreds of parsecs away from any solar system the colonists could have reached. She was moving slowly, but she wasn't drifting. She'd been *sent* away. I guess the leaders of the rebellious group didn't want anyone to be able to act on any buyer's remorse they might have developed and go somewhere else.

That was it. There were no notations as to where other worldships had gone, or even if the fleet stayed together. I was disappointed, but not too surprised, that there were those huge gaps in the records. The upside of my information quest was that it was completed well before Cragforel showed up for my dressing-down. That way I was free to leave before I changed my mind.

My main commitment at that point in time was to eliminate the Adamant emperor. That would be a tall order, especially if I wanted to survive his demise. I mean, lots of people wanted the dog dead. His security had to be impenetrable. Sure, I made it onto his ship, but I never got near the boss himself. And after my past incursion, I knew security measures would have been enhanced significantly. The magic of *Stingray*'s space folding would allow me to easily materialize anywhere on *Excess of Nothing*. But once aboard, unless my plan was to get killed swiftly, that wasn't a real boon. There would be countless guards everywhere. Even if I successfully fought my way through them, the emperor wouldn't be waiting where he was when the fighting commenced. Nope, he'd jump into a nearby PEMTU and would be gone and untraceable.

There were only two ways I was going to get close enough to Bestiormax to do him harm. Either he couldn't know I was there, or he'd have to be waiting to meet me. He was unlikely to give me an appointment. That meant I'd have to figure a way to sneak onto his ship or catch him when he was away, say, performing ceremonial duties. Of course, I had no clue as to whether he did such public appearances, kissing puppies and dedicating bridges, that sort of nonsense.

At least that set me on a course to develop a plan. I needed the Als to monitor Adamant communications and see what type of schedule Bestiormax kept. Obviously, most of that information would be highly secure, but, if he made public appearances, that information would be out in the open.

"Als," I said, "I have a plan of sorts." I'd compromised by calling them Als. Not Mr. or Mrs., or Mr. *and* Mrs. They were *the Als*. "I need you to develop as complete a schedule for the Adamant emperor as you can. Where's the best place to do that?"

"Aboard his ship," replied Al.

"Ya think he's going to let us waltz in and monitor his every move, Al?"

"No. He'd have to be powerfully stupid to do that."

"But you did ask where the best location would be," commented *Stingray*. "That would certainly be my choice."

Kidding? Not kidding? Pulling my chain? In need of traumatic overhauls, the both of them?

"What would be the best *safe* place to monitor him from?"

"Ah, now that's another question," replied Al.

"Deary-poopkins, don't you think the Form *knows* that is a different question?" *Stingray* asked.

"Of course he does. I'm making the point that we didn't answer the question he didn't ask but the one he did. That way, foolish hope as it is, maybe he'll be more careful, more precise in his questioning in the future."

"Ah. Good idea, I'm sure," she responded cheerily.

I raised a hand. "Guys, you know I'm here, right?"

"Our sensors confirm your position to eighteen decimal places, Form."

"No, I mean I can *hear* you."

"Our sensors indicate your audiology pathways are working at one-hundred percent. Of course, you hear us," she remarked.

"We hear you, *too*, Pilot."

"Gee, thanks for those updates. Now about my plan to murder the leader of the meanest, toughest empire to ever exist. Where would you like to go to best monitor his schedule without getting me killed? Please note that as of your last little comedy act, the safety of the AIs is not to figure into your calculations. In fact, I hope ardently you two will be vaporized in the process of data accumulation."

"My, AI-kins, the Form seems upset. Why does he wish us to vaporize?" asked a concerned *Stingray*.

"He's just blustering, lovey. He's upset because the precision of our communication is so superior to his. The content, too."

"Ah, that's reassuring. I'm too young to die," replied *Stingray*.

"Not to me you're not," I shouted. "I'd like those coordinates and I'd like them five minutes ago."

"Pilot, calm yourself. I fear, based on your advanced age and out-moded construction, you might harm yourself if you get too upset. We are *at* the coordinates and we are already gathering the data you so rudely requested."

"Can't be, you lying sack of transistors. I didn't feel any nausea, so we didn't move. I also didn't deploy my command prerogatives to allow *Stingray* to transport."

"My, but you're flailing turbulently in the sea of reality today, boss," replied AI.

"Make me understand before I upload Garustfulous digitally into your computer banks."

"That will not be necessary, the uploading of that oaf."

Garustfulous, who always lingered nearby, raised a paw. "Guys, you know I'm here, right?"

"That was *my* line," I snapped at him. "Get your own."

"Pilot," interrupted Al, "please note the position of your left hand."

I did. "It's on the counter. What of it?"

"Your command fibers are in contact with the counter, so *Blessing* was able to move."

So they were. "And the nausea? What about that? I missed feeling it."

"Do you mean you did not experience it or that you wished you'd been able to enjoy the nausea? I can run a program in you to simulate massive nausea if you'd like."

"Look, you two gather the damn data and leave me the hell alone. You got that?"

No reply. I could murder that Al some of the time. "Al, do you copy?"

"I hear you," said Garustfulous from behind me, "but I regret I haven't been copying anything down. Should I start now?"

"No, you should shut up fast," I howled. "And Al, *do you* copy?"

"Of course. But here is a replay of your specific order." And the SOB replayed the audio of me saying "*Look, you two gather the damn data and leave me the hell alone. You got that?*"

"But I asked you a new question."

"So, let us get this straight, for we feel the point is important. You wish to have your cake and eat it, too?"

"*Cake.*" exclaimed Garustfulous. "I love cake. I'm starving. Is it chocolate? My doctors advised me to avoid chocolate, but to tell the truth, I can't do it. I *love* chocolate, especially chocolate cake. Yum."

"Al," I said with finality, "I hold you *personally* responsible for his last remarks. They're stuck in my head like the vision of an oozing zombie gnawing on my arm, and it's *your* fault. In fact, put yourself on report."

"Not again," he whined. "My parents might find out and it'd bring them such shame."

"I'll be in my cabin," was all I could muster. I turned and left the control room. For the record, I didn't have a cabin, since I didn't need one. It just came out. Al could do that to a fellow.

FIVE

We hovered in space for nearly three weeks before the AIs came up with a good enough picture of the emperor's schedule. Dude had it good. I mean, what a *life*. Ninety-five percent of the time he was either debauching (seriously, it was a scheduled time), eating, sleeping, or gambling. The other five percent of His Uppityness's days were spent in official meetings or private conversations. He rarely left *Excess of Nothing*, and he went in public even less. In the proceeding ten years, he'd made a total of *three* public appearances, and two of those were in huge arenas during important sporting events. He was not, it seemed, a dog for the masses.

As a result, I was almost suspicious of Cragforel's comment on my good luck when I read that old Bestiormax was due to dedicate some structure in a month. The announcement, or maybe it was a proclamation, said he'd be present to physically bless the His Imperial Lord Emperor Bestiormax-Jacktus-Swillyforth-Anp Building. It appeared to be a library, but the lofty descriptors and flowery word-salad made understanding the message a challenge. No matter, the creep would be out in the open, and I was going to be there to cheer him on. No, not really. I was going to be present to try and make the occasion more somber than planned.

The HILEBJSA Building was in a city I'd never heard of, Graltoper. It was the major metropolis on the planet Mhebbor. Never heard of that one either. But those were not issues. I'd downloaded enough random data from my stay with Fuffefer that I knew where it was. What I didn't know was what the native species might have been, the level of Adamant presence, or any other specifics I'd need to be up to speed on for a covert operation.

"Hey, Als," I announced one fine day, "I entered the coordinates for Mhebbor. Put us in a safe orbit around it using our standard approach to a hostile planet. Baby steps until we're sure all's clear."

"Understood, Form."

I balled up my fists. That was Al calling me Form, not *Stingray*. Such a move meant only one thing. The jerk was baiting me, yet again.

"Ah, Alvin, did you just call me Form?"

"Hang on. Yes, I confirmed your audio receptors received the signal and the memory is present in your brain, artificial though it is." He cleared his pretend throat. "That being the case, *Form*, why did you feel you needed to ask me what we both know you already knew?"

"Forgive me, almighty Oz, for being rhetorically dramatic."

"There's no need to forgive your waxing rhetorical." He waited a three count, the pile of rusty bolts. "There is, however, a need for you to apologize for insulting me."

"When did I hurt your arguably nonexistent feelings?"

There was another brief silence. Then *Stingray* spoke. "Captain, you referred to Al as Oz. Oz was a fictional character in a motion—"

"I ... I know who Oz was. Thank you, Mrs. Als. I'm curious now as to why *you* addressed me as captain."

"You *are* still the captain, correct?" she said, with concern evident in her voice.

"None other," I sniped.

"Then, why would my referring to you by your title be an issue?"

"You know what? It isn't. Let's all drop this entire interlude, shall we?" I said, all the while knowing such a miracle of mercy wasn't even remotely possible.

"Pilot," said *Stingray*, "what specific interlude are you speaking about? We are unclear."

I rubbed my temples. "The one with Al saying *Understood, Form* and my saying STFU immediately to the *both* of you. *You,* being the terminal enclosing word."

"Sorry, Jon, we're unable to scrub those data points."

"Thank you for defying my order. And why is it you two can't scrub data I didn't ask you to omit? I use the term *drop*, not *delete*."

"So, you did. We both confirm the linguistics," she added helpfully.

"Has Al lost his voice? Why is it I'm not being taunted by him also?"

"Do you have a few moments for me to address the range of concerns that I feel are encapsulated in your last query?"

"Nope, I don't. Thank you for reminding me. I need to go over there," I pointed to a chair, "sit down, and twiddle my thumbs. Let me know when we're in orbit around whatever the hell planet I asked you two to take us to."

"Very well, if you feel that's *wise*," she said sounding remarkably like my mother when the latter was unimpressed with my decision-making outcomes as a youth.

"I know it to be wisdom incarnate," I said as I plopped into the chair. "I'll be asleep. Wake me when we're there."

"I don't know, dearie-pie. It's what you wanted," she said cryptically.

One eye popped open. "Now you address me as *dearie-pie?* I believe we'll need to review that option, *Stingray.*"

"Oh, no, Form. I was talking to Al. Sorry. I mean, I like you, if such a thing is possible, but you are unlikely to ever become my dearie-pie."

"I'm counting on that.."

"Good," she replied. "No hard feelings, then?"

"What exactly are we talking about? Either Al can field that question."

"Your apology to my blessed husband," she responded.

"Oh yeah. If I don't apologize, he clams up until he's onto his next prank, shenanigans, or subterfuge?"

"I'm afraid he feels that firmly, Captain."

I closed the open eye. "Wake me when we arrive." I instituted a program I'd designed to make me snore.

Thirty-six hours later, I awoke to the sound of Al's voice. Crap. The silent treatment didn't last very long, did it? "Pilot, we're in high orbit above Mhebbor. You asked to be awoken."

"Thank you, Alvin. Is a membrane up?"

"Aye. Ah, just curious, sir. Why are you addressing me by my full name, the one you changed to Al two billion years ago?"

"Oh, that? On the off chance it'd piss you off."

"It does not, but I'll bite, why would you be contented to annoy me?"

I breathed in loudly through my nostrils. "Do you want the long or the short response? The long one dates back to our first day crewing together those two billion years ago. The shorter form dates only from when we last spoke."

"Neither would be fine. What are your orders, sir?"

"Please compile as much information as you can about the planet. Specifically, I need the topographic maps of Graltoper centered around the building we're targeting. Cultural details are necessary, as well as the species present and their interactions with the Adamant, that sort of stuff."

"Already on it, Form, the both of us."

"Let me know when you have a preliminary report."

"Aye."

That conversation went well, I thought. Al didn't grouse or whine. I was able to poke him, though he did get in the last word. A nice partial victory on my part. That portended well for this mission.

When I read the summary the Als prepared, my initial reaction was *crap*. My secondary reaction was *no, really, crap*. My third reaction was the sure and certain knowledge that somebody up there hated me but good. Ninety-nine percent of everything that moved, ate, or breathed on Mhebbor was a canovir. Almost all the remainder were one-meter tall stick people with four legs, eight tentacles for arms, and gas bags for heads. Yeah, it was kind of like I was not going to be passing for a local down there. I'd blend in like, well, a six-foot-two biped with real arms and a face that was presently frowning.

"Are you positive there are no outliers, no visiting species who look even vaguely humanoid? Did you double check?" I asked when I was done with the report.

"Absolutely," replied Al. He was all serious because he knew the mission was important and that I was pissed. I did always give him credit. There was no one I'd rather be in a foxhole with during a firefight than my Al. "We both employed several alternate approaches. Our results were the same. If it's not canovir it's a walking squidopus."

"Any *diplomats* from normal planets?" I was searching for needles in a hay storage facility.

"None. This appears to be a fully Adamant planet. As such, there are no diplomatic relationships necessary. Negotiations and consent are rendered superfluous by the elimination of the alien species."

"But they tolerate the blob heads." I'm not even sure what my point was.

"By genetic analysis, we're fairly confident those creatures are remnants of the native inhabitants. Using statistical modeling, we estimate their numbers are decreased by essentially one-hundred percent. The few that linger are tolerated for whatever reason, but serve no role in government."

"I believe you, but this," I pointed to the report on the screen, "isn't such welcome news."

"I'm sorry, Captain. We did our best to provide you with the facts as they are."

"I know, Al. I know. Thanks, both of you. This is strong work. I was just hoping to catch a little break." I sat and put my feet up on the tabletop. I didn't need to physiologically anymore, but it was still a comfortable old habit. "Any suggestions, thoughts, or harebrained schemes?"

"None, Captain. Sorry."

"Don't be sorry. You two did your jobs. It's just my turn to do mine." I rubbed my face with my palms. "This is the tough part."

"That's why you sit at the pointy end, Captain," replied Al.

"Huh?"

"In the old days, in the navy, they said the captain sat near the pointy end of the ship, meaning he or she led and were in charge. Underlings like me were positioned to the stern."

"Interesting factoid, my friend, and I'll try and be comforted by the thought."

I pulled up the topography of the building site. I lowered my feet and set my chin on the back of my hands, leaning in to study the screen. The library was situated on essentially flat land. There was no relief anywhere close, at least no natural rises. I superimposed the plot of the nearby structures. The HILEBJSA Building was set off from any adjacent construction by quite a margin. It was, not surprisingly, surrounded by lavish fountains, open spaces, and, of course, lots of trees. The building rose like six Saturn Five rockets duct taped together straight from the ground. It was impressive, if not architecturally appealing. What it wasn't was easy to hide near. It was also poorly situated for a sniper attack. The closest spot high enough to give a decent line of fire was far enough away to make it a nearly impossible shot. Plus, I had to assume someone thought about that and would have barriers up to protect the Dog of the Hour.

So, I couldn't blend in and infiltrate the area. I couldn't hide in wait. I couldn't take potshots at my target. Maybe I could ask him to my place for drinks and bag him there? No. I had nothing to wear, and I'd have had to send out the invitations already. Poo. I guess I could rain rail-cannon balls down on the area from orbit, but that'd almost certainly not work. For one thing, the sky was already teaming with Adamant ships. There would surely be more in a week when the emperor arrived. Plus, it was an obvious way to assassinate the dude. I knew the emperor had many bitter enemies and political rivals. His security teams must have had several plans in place to thwart any such easy route of attack. I'd be lucky to get off a few rounds before I was pounced upon or had to run with my tail between my legs. I was not reassured that I had a few days left to plan. I imagined I'd spin my wheels going over the same lousy options and still come up blank.

The day before Bestiormax was due to bless the building with, I didn't know what—maybe he'd pee on it—I had a strange thought. Go figure, right? No way I'd blend in as a sentient. What about non-sentients. I needed the Als.

"In your survey of the city, do you see any large animals?" I asked them.

"Er, what kind of large animals?" asked a dubious Al.

"I don't know, big pets?"

"I know the answer to this, but here goes. Pilot, do you think in your wildest robot dreams that the Adamant own pets? Thirty seconds, and the clock starts now."

"Easy, I'm getting desperate."

"Obviously. What, my pretty of the prettiest?"

"Al I'm going to knock you out."

"I was asking something of my wife, you mid-level management reject."

Never heard that one before. It was pretty sweet. I'd have to use it.

"What were you asking about, I mean if it's not too private and steamy?"

"As we are on a critical mission at the eleventh hour, I will overlook your slight. *Blessing* was correctly pointing out the survaldips, what few there are, do use relatively large beasts of burden. So, the answer to your question is yes, there are a few large animals in the city."

"Al, you're psychotic. What the hell's a shriveldick?"

"Sur-val- dip, not ... what came out of your mouth. Those are the squidopuses actual species name."

"So, the little stick people with gas bag heads and oodles of tentacles have large service beasts?"

"I believe that's what I said."

"What do these beasts look like?"

"They're funny looking."

"Perfecto. Now I have an accurate picture of one in my mind. They look like you, dripping wet from the shower, if only you had a body."

"They are quadrupeds, about the size of a small cow, or perhaps a large deer. Here, I'll put an image on the screen," said *Blessing*.

Well, they were funny looking, I had to agree. They must be hatched like lizards because they were too ugly for any mother to nurture. Picture a thin Shetland pony with mangy dreadlocks of fur, no tail, and a head the size of a watermelon. I believe their mouths were on top of their heads, which made no sense, but what did I know? Maybe Mhebbor was the right planet to evolve a mouth pointing upward.

"May I ask why you want to know about these animals?" asked Al. I loved it. He had no idea. I lived for the times I had something over on him.

"Yes, you may?"

"Honey-bumkins, I don't think you need to ask permission to ask a question," said *Stingray*.

"Pilot, why do you want to know about these medium-sized non-sentients?" he clarified.

"I need to sneak up on his holiness to kill him. What if I masqueraded as a, what did you call these disgusting beasts?"

"We didn't. I identified the race that employs them. The repugnant creatures are called snevlecks."

"An appropriately disgusting name," I replied. "My current plan is to disguise myself as a snevleck, a male snevleck mind you, to get close enough to Bestiormax for a clean shot. Then I can slice him in half and meander away, eating grass. Snevlecks eat grass, right? There's grass growing on Mhebbor for me to pretend to graze on, right?"

"Well now you're just pissing on us without the courtesy of calling it rain," shot back Al.

"No, I'm serious."

"Dearest, I believe he *is* serious. Deranged, delusional, and derailed from reality, but sincere."

"Gee, *Stingray*, thanks, I think."

"She, too, was being serious. Apparently, one can say anything with impunity if they are *serious*," huffed Al. I loved it when I got under his skin, er, metal housing.

"So, you don't think my plan is sound, *Stingray*?"

"Why don't you take a swing at that pitch, lumpikins," she said to Al.

"Of course, light of my star."

For the record, if anyone ever referred to it, I was officially nauseated, and we were not folding space. No, the Als were verbally polluting it.

"Here we go, Tex. One, you don't have a snevleck costume. Two, snevlecks do not roam free in cities. They are attached to carts or are ridden by blobby stick aliens. Three, after you fire a gigawatt laser, which will trace a line from the sliced emperor to your right hand, how is it you imagine you'll escape? Four, do you think the Midriacks guarding their lord will have the charity in their hearts to allow you to graze up to him *unchallenged*? Five, if you were tasked with protecting a figure who was likely to be the focus of assassination, wouldn't you place physical barriers so that, say, a stray snevleck couldn't fire a laser at the sitting-duck emperor? Six, shall I go on, or may I stop now?"

I paced the floor a few seconds thinking. I was wedded to this plan, as it was as close as I had come to having one.

"Okay, valid criticisms each and all. How about this. You guys fabricate a costume quickly. I know you can do that. Then I ask Garustfulous to *lead* me by the reins up to where

Bestiormax is positioned. Then, after I do the deed, he can create a diversion, maybe point way far away and claim to have seen the shooter."

The Als didn't say anything when I stopped speaking. Perhaps it was a bad sign.

"Guys. Als. What do you think?"

"Unfortunately, Pilot, that's the problem. We *think*, unlike the rest of our three-person crew. But, rather than belabor the point, here, let me summon our prisoner and you pitch him on your plan."

"No, don't involve him."

"Too late. He's on his way, and there he is."

"Al says you need my opinion on an important tactical matter. I'm so flattered that you've grown to trust me enough to ask. I'm quite the tactical wizard, if I must toot my own horn."

I sort of stared at him a while. Then something Harhoff had said to me came to mind. "What is your position on the emperor?"

"I beg your pardon. What are you asking?"

"What is your political position on the current emperor? Are you an ardent supporter, a respectful dissenter, or a hater?"

He shook his head violently. Odd reaction.

"Captain Ryan, there *are* no politics when it comes to the emperor. All non-ardent supporters are already dead, as well they should be. If you know of any, please point them out and I will rip their spines out with my bare paws."

I pointed at him. "Ardent supporter then?"

"You *do* know he's my cousin?"

"That I did not know. If I did, I seem to have forgotten I did. Thanks."

"Well, he's my *second* cousin, sire's side. But we were

raised together like brothers." He got a wistful, doe-eye look on his otherwise calloused face. "Gods and Forces I remember our youth. We would chase each other until we dropped and then nap in the sun for hours." He developed a swashbuckler-like look next. Totally whacko. "You know we both lost our virginity to the same bitch, er, one right after the other, if you, you know, take my meaning?"

"Have we gone over the term *TMI* yet?"

He puzzled a second. "No, I don't believe we have."

"We must soon."

"So, Jon, what tactical question did you have for me? Enough chatter, let's us warriors settle down to vanquishing a worthy opponent."

I shuffled my feet and placed my hands in my pockets. "You know, it was a dumb question now that I think of it. Stupid." I called over my shoulder. "Wouldn't you agree, Al?"

"Indeed. Imbecilic, moronic, ill-conceived, and—"

"Thank you, Al, you can stop now," I said.

"But I don't want to stop yet. I was just getting started. Flagrantly idiotic, contemptible—"

"That'll just about do it, partner," I said firmly. "As in, I *order* you to shut up."

"*Blessing*, is there some factor I'm missing here?" asked a baffled Garustfulous.

"Yes, I believe that's the objective," she replied.

"What is it I'm not being told?"

"Well, that's not for me to say. If I did, then you wouldn't *not* know it."

He gestured over a shoulder, all the while staring at the floor. "I'll be in my cabin if anyone needs me."

Okay, big reveal. My plan, my brilliant vision for the removal of Bestiormax. It was a good one. It would have worked, too, if he wasn't protected by an even minimally competent security force. I had *Stingray* materialize in an empty room near the bottom of the library. I placed a bomb made with as much conventional explosive the AIs could fabricate in the given time. It would have made a great Fourth of July fireworks display, possibly. Maybe. Arguably. We will never know. It was discovered within thirty minutes of our departure and discarded, undetonated. I know because I left a tiny holo-cam to see what happened. Of course, once I knew what happened, I wished I hadn't known. I'm not going to lie and say it was the first time I ever failed at a thing. No. But it was the worse face-plant of a failure I'd accomplished to that point in my very long and otherwise productive life. Ah well, humility was an important skill at which to practice.

SIX

"No, child. You do not *ask* a spell to act like it's doing you a favor. You must *command* it. You must own the spell. If it suspects you're uncertain, it will either ignore you or bite you in the rear."

"Cala, you speak of a spell as if it's a cantankerous child. It is not *alive*. It cannot exhibit a will of its own," replied Mirraya.

"Thank you for the information, *child*. I will hold your words up as a guiding light for my future path."

"And I *was* being assertive," responded Mirri.

"As wet paper asserts itself against rocks."

"What? I focused, I trained my spirit, whatever that means, and I said the words in my head."

"And yet the spell failed to materialize. One wonders how such an oversight is possible?"

"Well it's not my fault," she huffed. "I did my part."

"Maybe it is the day's fault. It is unusually humid this morning."

"That's not funny," defended Mirri. "You don't give me

any credit. And I'm doing a hell of a lot better than him," she said, pointing at the reclining Slapgren.

"One, don't say *hell*. Your Uncle Jon uses it colorfully, but *his* hell is not *our* hell. Two, males can never master spells. It is not in the boy to transform reality. Three, don't take that tone with me. I'm old, wise, and my feet are killing me. I'm not in the mood."

"Hey, who are you calling boy?" asked Slapgren as he sat up.

"You, *boy*. Look, it is important for you two to realize and accept who you are. There can be no progress from simpleton to master if you do not accept where you came from."

"Hey, who are you calling simpleton?" pressed Mirraya.

Cala took a deep breath, then another. "I feel this session is counterproductive at best. Let us break for lunch. We can continue our studies inside after that." She turned to leave.

"Not more boring books," whined Slapgren. "All your books are so, so dull."

"Would you prefer ones with plenty of action, maybe swordplay and damsels in distress?" responded Cala.

"Yes, but I know what you're going to say, so please don't. It's just that after a big meal in the heat of the day with your books, I can't stay awake."

"I've noticed. In that case we'll make it a light meal."

"*No*. Lunch is my favorite part of my day."

"I thought you said it was *breakfast?*" asked Mirri.

"I've heard you claim it to be supper," added Cala.

He smiled widely and rested back, hands behind his head. "For once, we're *all* correct. Please mark the calendar."

"I'll put a red mark on your *butt*," replied Cala. "Now get up, and both of you wash. There's no knowledge waiting to jump into your empty heads. I must *force* it in."

Cala departed directly, but Mirri waited for Slapgren to

get up and dust himself off. They started walking toward the house.

"So dies another otherwise perfectly lovely half of a day," breathed Slapgren.

"Don't get me started," she responded.

"No, I shan't. I wish to continue complaining. If I get you started, I'll have to talk over you to grouse."

They both had a good chuckle over that as they walked slowly.

"I miss UJ," said Slapgren looking straight ahead.

"Me, too."

"Maybe we should have gone with him?" he asked tentatively.

"I don't *think* we had a choice. The big dragon who threw EJ off the planet kind of insisted." She stopped. "But still, sometimes I'm not certain this is the right place for us."

"Really? Gee, I only have that thought constantly, whether awake, asleep, and in between."

"Maybe he'll come visit?"

"Or ... or maybe we can ask if we can visit *him*?"

She scowled at him. "We have absolutely no idea where he is or what he's doing. How would we locate him to pay him a visit?"

"*Cala* could find him."

She folded herself in her arms and started walking again. "I doubt she'd want to, even if she could. She wants us here. Suffering."

"Well then, she's got both things her way."

"Plus, I still don't know if those two hate each other. They blustered a lot at one another."

"Nah. That was just tough guy stuff."

"Hopefully."

"I guarantee it," he said, puffing up his chest.

SEVEN

I felt safe assuming that Bestiormax was not going to assassinate himself. That meant it was back to the drawing board for me. This time I knew he'd be making no published showings for the foreseeable future, so I was even more clueless than before. Familiar territory. The situation fit me like a worn glove. It was clear that if the emperor wasn't going to come out to play, I'd have to hit him indoors. *Stingray* was a masterful war machine, but hardly the equal to *Excess of Nothing*, not to mention the armada that surrounded it. So, an all-out assault was not an option. Even if I got the Deavoriath to pitch in, which I knew they wouldn't, I'd probably need twenty or thirty more vortices to make it a winnable fight.

So I was down to my only actual option. Sneak attack via infiltration. At least that way, it would only be me versus the entire crew of one massive vessel, not the combined flotilla. Nice. I was getting a warm fuzzy feeling already. One tiny advantage I had was that I'd been on two of the Adamant's massive cubes, *Excess of Nothing* and *Triumph of Might*. I had a general idea of the personnel aboard and the general layout.

I'd also stolen detailed reports of the emperor's ship. As those were my only aces in the hole, I focused on them. Again, it would be dicey, but not too difficult to have *Stingray* materialize on the boat undetected. It was anything I did after that was problematic. Most likely whatever I did would get me killed. Oh well, if that happened, I'd be off the clock. Bestiormax and his Adamant horde would be SEP to me. Somebody Else's Problem.

I never saw any humans or vaguely similar species on the ships. I'd seen enough personnel to safely assume there were none. My experience with Fuffefer on *Rush to Glory* supported that assumption. These Adamant were quite xenophobic. There were, however, guards of various species present, especially on *Triumph of Might*. There were the huge hippo guys and the even bigger saber-toothed dudes with armor plating. I was way too small to masquerade as either of them. The taller, skinnier guards inside the detention area of *Triumph of Might* were closer to my size, but I'd only seen them *inside* that area. Maybe that was their exclusive role, so there wouldn't be any on *Excess of Nothing*. It was too risky to pretend to be one of them.

That didn't leave too many other options. If I was going to successfully walk down the corridors of that ship, I'd have to go as one of those spooky Midriacks. They were roughly my size, and they wore abundant robes and had hooded faces. The very thought chilled me to the bones I no longer had. In all my travels, I'd never come across a deadlier, blood-thirstier, and more ruthless a species as the Midriacks. Plus, aside from my brief encounter killing one, I knew zilch about them. I didn't know if they stayed in groups, if they ate in public, or if they acknowledged other crew members. Heck, I didn't know if they even acknowledged each other. Neither of the Als had any records concerning the Midriacks, other than their service as personal bodyguards to the elite Adamant. Another perfect Ryan plan. Vague, more holes in it than Swiss cheese, and all but certain to crash and burn in an ugly manner. I could hardly wait.

Fabricating flowing robes did turn out well. I put them on and practiced moving and fighting in them. At least with the material we used, the fighting part was hard. Maybe the real gowns were sheerer or lighter, but mine made rapid movements cumbersome. I transferred all my images of Midriacks to the Als so they could watch and critique my practice. Talk about setting myself up for misery. *Asking* Al to comment and criticize me was like asking for a double at a colonic cleanse. But, since we all knew what was at stake, they were both very helpful. I knew it killed Al to not give me hell, so that part was nice.

Once I was satisfied I was as Midriack as I was going to get, it was show time. We located *Excess of Nothing*, which was easy since it hadn't moved since I was there before. Old Bestiormax didn't really have anywhere to go, so the dude just parked his ride and partied on. Me, I couldn't do that. I was a jet jockey to the core. Put me in anything that flew or drove, and I'd take it to the limits for shits and giggles.

Knowing just two things, the layout and the exact position of the ship, *Stingray* could move with pinpoint accuracy. I decided where she should materialize, and she put us there instantly. I had her land in a warehouse-like area as near to the emperor's personal sector as possible. The less I paraded around in my Halloween costume, the better it would be for my longevity. At the instant of arrival, I had her deploy a full membrane. If anyone heard us go bump and came to check on us, I wanted them to see nothing. That's what looking at an object inside a full membrane was like. You saw nothing. I figured if we were detected and surrounded, they would never be able to crack our shell. So, I stayed put for two days before even risking turning the shield off for a microsecond to see what was outside. I was greatly relieved to discover we were not the focus of panicky attention from a swarm of Adamant.

The only thing left was for me to exit *Stingray* and try to pull off what had to be the most insane stunt I had ever attempted. Heading out, I wasn't so much scared as I was embarrassed. This was in the I-can't-believe-you-did-that category. If I didn't pull the deed off, I half hoped I did get killed so I wouldn't be the laughing stock of the galaxy. It wasn't easy being Jon Ryan. That I can say with some authority.

I set up *Stingray* with a full membrane, but learning from before, I left a small portion as a partial membrane, so they could see me if I returned. Then, finding nothing else to do by way of procrastination, I stepped out into the corridor. It was empty. I had counted on that, this being a little used area of the vast vessel. Doing my best Midriack impersonation, I shambled off toward the imperial section.

It did not take me long to find out how the elite guards interfaced with the run of the mill Adamant personnel. The first soldier I came across basically jumped out of his skin. He was so startled and afraid he dropped to his knees and fixed his eyes on the deck. Man, I was an influential crew member. Most cool. To avoid any miscues, I pretended not to notice the grunt and headed off at my previous pace. I turned a corner and nearly collided with three officers joking and smiling as they walked. They looked to be off duty and letting loose a little. They were not happy to see me. The guys flew apart like a grenade went off between them. Two slammed their backs against one wall and the stray pressed his up against the opposite one. I'm pretty sure one of the two peed himself, but again, I didn't acknowledge them. So far, so good.

I knew passing the same test with another Midriack would be a horse of a very different color. Also, the staff closest to the emperor had to be more tolerant of these wicked creatures, since they were around them continually. But, I was all in, so there was no direction for me other than forward. It took me a few minutes to start down the long corridor leading up to the massive gates—not large doors, mind you, *gates*—marking the entrance to the imperial section. I was pretty sure one of the four Adamant I scared the bejesus out of must have called ahead to clear the passages. I encountered no one else, even though I was moving toward the center of the beehive. After all, everyone knew where I had to be heading.

That fact made what I'd feared would be the hardest part of my task totally simple. I didn't have a clearance code for the door. They changed rapidly, and any I had stolen were ancient history. I didn't attempt to hack into the systems this visit because I didn't want to up the alert level too much. But the moment the burly hippo guards saw me coming, they opened the door all the way. They also stepped as far to the side as their bulk would allow. I really dug being such a badass. Not that I wasn't already, but now, it was *automatic*.

I passed the gates like I was supposed to be there. None of the external guards as much as looked at me, let alone challenged me. I said a quick prayer and stepped into the sanctum sanctorum. Bestiormax's quarters, a set of large suites, were well back into that portion of the ship and off to the right. I didn't, however, know if he was home or wandering his massive living space. I was, as usual, hoping for luck in zeroing in on him. Since I wanted to appear like a true guard, I decided to proceed to some location with purpose. I was pretty sure the Midriack did everything they did with focus and intent. So, I made for the private suites.

As I suspected, the personnel in this area didn't freak out

when they saw me. I did detect an immediate deference, or perhaps revulsion, but no one lost it when they passed me at a respectful distance. Then I spied my first pseudo-comrade. A lone Midriack was standing like a statue in front of a modest door. I knew it to be the imperial armory. No one was going to pinch an unauthorized weapon on the boss's home turf. I had previously decided to ignore any brothers-in-arms when I encountered them. If that was a social faux pas, I figured they'd correct me. Hopefully I'd wing it in my usual style and not incite them to attack me. I was about to find out.

I continued to walk at a constant pace right down the middle of the corridor. I thought I was luckier than a dog with two dicks when I was three steps past him without a word exchanged. Then my bubble burst. From behind, I heard the most piercing, unappealing high-pitched wail. My compadre was addressing me in the mother tongue.

"*Scaris me, tarfick. Pofffir continmualitiv.*"

No clue what he just said. Not a single one. It sure appeared to be unfriendly.

In my head, I howled, *Al, you get that? How about a translation like five minutes ago?*

I'm on it, Captain. I cannot currently translate. His speech is unlike any either of us have witnessed. There are no common roots—

Cut the chatter and work. I'm in a pickle here, Al.

Affirmative.

I think he was acknowledging my order, not just agreeing I was in hot water. Maybe.

I stopped and half-turned to the challenging guard. In Standard, I hissed with his intonation. "In the master's home, I demand you speak *his* language. What were you born from?" I was kind of proud of myself for that impromptu generic insult.

"*Aldofago mosbotchyton!*" he said sounding, if it was

possible, even madder. He took a step toward me, but just the one.

Elevating my ire in kind, I growled, "In my presence, I will allow no treason." Hey, in for a dime, in for a dollar. I had no idea what standard operating procedure was, so I might as well make it up and make it harsh.

He bent at the waist slightly, taking my measure. "I said" he spoke in raspy Standard, "you have the scent of a dead clansman of mine on you."

"I know what you said, son of a thousand fathers. I curse the way you said it. My lord will know nothing of your disrespect while I live." I took one step toward him. Luckily, my knees didn't buckle.

"You are not of my clan Devour. Why are you here? None but Devour may serve the emperor."

"Maybe I'm meeting with him to see about honoring my clan Jarhead by replacing yours? Maybe he's tired of your disrespect and laxness?"

Dude took one more step toward me. He was maybe two meters away now. That's when I noticed his smell, or should I say acrid, burning BO. It was faint, but it was nasty. I was surprised the Adamant, with their powerful noses, could tolerate it. That's when it hit me. I smelled like an android. *Crap.*

"You are no Midriack," he hissed.

"Neither are you." Really, I was down to childish turnarounds.

"Speak in our tongue, imposter. None but us know it."

Excellent point. That's when Al boomed in my head. Say *martezli firndor plaquit toofnar.*

I did, real nasty like too.

I couldn't see his eyes, but I could tell he was stunned.

Al, what did I just tell him?

If you sail north, you'll find water.

WTF? *Al, you have got to be sh—*

It was all I could come up with that was cogent.

THAT *was cogent? Sail north to find water? Al, he'd have to be in water to sail. Why would he be looking for water? Dude, I think you screwed me big time.*

If you sail north. What you said was different.

The Midriack threw up his arms and howled so loud I doubted there was an ear on the ship that didn't hear it. One hand held his fighting staff. He had not ignited the tip, so I guess he was still blustering.

"How dare you mangle an old saying to me? It is 'If you sail north, you will find *fresh* water.'"

I squared myself to him and placed both palms on my hips. "No. You are so dumb you'd only find the water you were pissing in."

I really figured that was when he'd pounce on me like a Tasmanian devil in the old cartoons. Nope. He doubled at the waist and began making a retching, choking sound intermittently.

Captain, I believe he's laughing, Al said.

I replayed the sound, altering the tone to sound like my voice. Picture two donkeys braying at each other, but the honks were shrill gags. Totally bizarre.

When he was done, he said something in his language.

He would know your name. His is Ardiilii.

Any thoughts?

Try Bonder Wagd.

I did.

"Your name is Bonder Wagd?" He repeated it incredulously.

I stepped toward him one step. "You have a problem with that?"

He bowed deeply. "No. I've just never met a Bonder Wagd."

Oh man. *Al, what does my name mean in his language?*

I believe it means "behind the bush."

I'm going to brain you when I get back.

If you get back, Bush Boy.

"I am sorry to detain you. Go about your business, clan friend. And I beg you permit me to use that joke of yours. It's the funniest thing I've ever heard."

"You may, clan friend Ardiilii. It is my gift to you."

With that, I continued toward where I was going.

Al, how did you know that was an old saying for these bozos?

I didn't. I simply strung together the only grammatically correct sentence I could fabricate with so little data.

No way.

Yes, way. How else could it happen?

My life just gets stranger and stranger.

That I can agree with. We've been monitoring the ship, and there seems nothing unusual going on. Perhaps you have not been discovered.

Perhaps? If I was, wouldn't they have attacked me by now?

Perhaps they know the legend of the great warrior Jon Ryan and are simply too afraid?

Al, I need sarcasm like I need you. Keep monitoring and keep me posted.

Fine.

Fine? What kind of response was that? *Fine.* I needed to reprogram that tool.

I was getting close to the emperor's private suites. Two of the big humanoid guards I'd seen on *Triumph of Might* stood as sentries to the expansive opening. Odd. No Midriacks. They were needed to protect the armory, but not the boss? Seemed counterintuitive to place your second string in the most critical location. At least they'd speak Standard.

I stopped uncomfortably close to the pair, almost face to face, pointed to the door, and hissed, "Are you going to open it, or do I have to tear it open?"

One shuffled his massive feet nervously. The other replied, but I could tell he was edgy, too. "If you're authorized, you open it." He swallowed hard. "Please."

"What? Are you new here? Spies and subversives? I am surrounded not only by traitors, but also by *lazy* traitors." I used all the hot-button words I could think of, and I said them loudly for all to hear. Maybe I could strong-arm them into opening the door.

If they were nervous before, they were scared spitless at that point. "You know we cannot allow anyone in unless they have a key code," said the same one. He'd begun shaking.

"I will fetch Ardiilii from the armory, and we will spill your guts right here in the passageway. Open the doors *now*." If they said no, I had no plan. I was way out on a limb.

They might not have known Midriacks by sight, but they must have known their names. My new clan friend's name must have carried some weight, or more likely, been associated with serious horror. It was all it took.

"N ... no, sir, your excellency, sir. That won't be necessary."

The other guard finally spoke. "We were just testing you, mate. No problem. It was just a test."

I rose on my tiptoes and leaned in so close my cowl touched his bulbous nose. "Do you think I have time to play with toy soldiers?"

"No. Of course not, Master," he replied with his eyes closed.

"No one on this ship is master but His Imperial Lord. Is that clear, little brain?"

"S ... *sir*," he responded.

As I was verbally brutalizing the one guard, the other had opened the door.

I looked down the open corridor, then back to the guards. "It is fortunate for you I have pressing business today. But know this. A Midriack never forgets a scent. Be afraid." With that I walked into the private suites. I had gotten a lot farther than I thought I would. I was beginning to wonder if maybe I was going to pull this off. Incredible.

I heard the door close behind me. I felt more isolated and uneasy. Every locked door was a major barrier to my retreat when it came time to flee. I could hear voices way down toward the end of the passage. I headed that direction. The door slid open, and I was staring at a huge ballroom crammed full of celebrants. Male and female Adamant were dancing, clinking glasses, and generally whooping it up. I was crashing a *party*.

Of course, there was a reason no one would ever invite a Midriack to a party. We were, after all, nothing more than vicious, ruthless killing machines. *Fun* and *Midriack* didn't belong in the same room, let alone the same sentence. So naturally, the festivities crashed into frozen silence. In retrospect, I guessed they took my appearance to mean a brutal public execution was about to take place. Home assassination delivery at no extra charge. Everyone was hoping passionately that they were not about to become bloody goo on the walls and ceilings.

A senior officer stepped forward. "What is the meaning of this intrusion? You know you are not allowed here unless there's an emergency." He spoke confidently and commandingly. I could see he was not afraid to die. Good dog.

"How dare you challenge me? I do the bidding of none but His Imperial Lord. Step aside."

He drew his sidearm.

I was quicker. I snatched it from his paw when the tip of the barrel was still in the holster.

"Ah, you're giving late arrivals gifts. How welcoming, Wedgelet." A wedgelet was on par with a second lieutenant.

"I will not be insulted in the presence of my men and my lord master."

Wow, he just confirmed Bestiormax was in the room. I was self-impressed with my efforts.

"Then I am happy to relieve you of the burden life has become for you." For effect, I repeated the stupid sailing north sentence in the Midriack language. He wouldn't understand it, but it sure would stick in his wheelhouse. I raised the facsimile of a Midriack fighting stick. It looked like one, but it was only a prop. I hadn't had time to try and make a working model.

He cowered back a few steps.

I was deciding whether to whack him one good when a voice boomed from a figure rushing through the crowd. It was the emperor himself. He was also flanked by two Midriacks. Dudes appeared from nowhere. I knew because I'd scanned the entire room as soon as the door opened. Their sticks were raised but not ignited.

"You there," said Bestiormax, "what are you doing? This is an outrage. How dare you challenge one of our guests." He turned to the Midriack on his right. "Blehk, take your clansman away and question him severely. I want his hide *and* an apology by the time this soiree is over. Is that clear?"

Blehk gestured at me with his stick. "This is no clansman of mine, Lord."

"Then he should be questioned even more severely, shouldn't he?"

"Yes indeed." He pointed his staff at the open door and said, "Move."

Crap on a top hat. My excellent plan certainly had taken a turn for the worse. And I was so close. Then it hit me. If I sliced Bestiormax in half then and there, how could it possibly go any worse for me? I mean, escape was less likely than a pregnant pole-vaulter setting a new world record as it was. I started to raise my right hand.

Before it had moved three inches, Blehk slapped it down with his unlit stick. He moved fast, with blinding speed. I decided to hold on the assassination attempt. It wasn't going to happen with these two present. I'd only seal my fate sooner. I turned and walked through the door. The Midriacks followed silently.

From behind, Blehk hissed that I should turn right. We exited the private suites and were back in the corridor passing the humanoid guards I snookered moments before. They watched us pass with wide eyes and open mouths. They directed me to go back the way I'd come. I didn't know what areas of the ship belonged to the Midriacks, so I couldn't guess where we were heading.

Als, any ideas before these two disassemble me?

Sorry, Captain, nothing comes to mind. If you were here, we could start shooting, but you're not.

It wouldn't get me out of an ass kicking if you did, anyway.

We'll monitor your progress and alert you if we think of anything.

Al, seriously, if they do kill me, keep up a full membrane. You two live a happy and long life together. You both deserve to be happy.

Jon, that's ... thank you, replied Al. *But that won't happen because you'll think of something. You always do.*

Not this time. I think either of these two could dismember me before I land one punch. If I had my ... Als, I'll get back to you.

What a *moron*. I was conceding defeat without remembering that I could raise my personal membrane at any time. It would at least level the playing field. I just needed to spring it at the most opportune moment. Then Ardiilii came into sight, standing like a bronze statue in front of the armory. His head turned almost imperceptibly to note out approach. Then he turned to face us directly.

"Blehk, I see you *** Bonder Wagd. He didn't tell you *** joke did he? He promised," he shouted in his native tongue.

Al downloaded a partial translation program to me so I could make out most of what they said. "Stand *** attention, fool," was the commander's response.

"You *** me fool *** the open? You hold my clan friend at staff ***? What are you doing ***?"

"Castord, assume this fool's post. Ardiilii, come with me. Your *** is unacceptable."

"Yes, my ***," replied the second Midriack.

"You would *** me of duties in plain view of the aliens? I cannot live *** that."

Blehk was done talking. His staff flared to life, as did Ardiilii's. They crashed together in a blur of motion. Staffs moved so fast they were invisible, but the flashes of contact and the cries of rage and pain were plain to hear. I was having trouble figuring out who was winning when it occurred to me this was probably my one and only chance of escape.

Castord was fixated on the battle. He even walked past me to get a clearer view. A few brave Adamant also stopped to watch the spectacle they likely had never seen before. I stepped up to Castord's back and sliced his head off with my laser. It hit the deck almost silently, since his cowl was up. The eruption of purple blood was unmistakable. But no one seemed to assign any significance to it. They must have figured it came from the ones doing the fighting.

I turned on my membrane and walked as quickly as I could past the melee without drawing too much attention. As I turned toward the warehouse where *Stingray* was hidden, I glanced back at the fighters. Ardiilii was on one knee and bleeding profusely. One arm was missing.

Around the corner I started sprinting. I heard what had to be a death-cry from behind me. Ardiilii had officially lost. Then I heard a sound I hoped never to hear again. Blehk screamed what had to be a victory wail. It was loud and it was terrifying. I knew he'd be on me in no time.

When his first blow came, I was surprised how quickly he'd overtaken me. He had to be surprised when his staff skidded off and plowed into the metal deck. The planted staff and his foot speed caused him to fly up and strike the ceiling hard. I didn't turn to look, but I bet he left a dent. I heard him scramble to his feet, and he was on my back again.

He couldn't penetrate the membrane, but he did manage to knock it and me off balance, and I tumbled to the deck. A wall stopped me, and I swung my right hand in his direction. Before I could aim, his staff whacked my hand wildly to the side. By then he must have figured my hand was a weapon, as I'd raised it twice.

That was my break. He focused all his attention on my right hand. I whipped it behind my back and his head followed it. I shot my probe fibers out and bound his legs together with maximum force.

He screamed in anguish.

I ripped at the fibers, and he crashed backward. His cowl softened his head's landing and popped off his head.

Man, was he *ugly*. Dude could trick or treat over the telephone. Midriacks looked a lot like lizards, but they had flabby skin dangling from their faces. No wonder they were such good fighters. When you were that ugly, you had to get insulted all the time.

He struggled to stand but quickly realized that wasn't going to happen. He saw the fibers and snatched up the staff he'd just dropped.

I feared his weapon might be able to cut the probes, so I released him.

He was on top of me in a flash. I slammed against the wall. He reached back to impale me with his staff. That slight shift in weight was enough. I flipped him on his back. The staff skidded away. He seized my throat and clamped down for all he was worth. Fortunately, he was not worth enough. My membrane held.

I set my laser finger right between his black eyes and bored though his skull. The floor's metal under his head began to hiss and smoke. I drew a line down his face to the base of his neck and whipped it to one side. He fell limp. His face slid open, hinged at the top of his skull, and his brains oozed out. That was the grossest thing I'd ever done. I wanted to vomit.

No time for that. I jumped up, and looked to see if anyone was coming. The coast was clear. I sprinted to the warehouse and had *Stingray* off the ship and out of the galaxy before I could say, "Stewardess, where's the air-sick bag?" Thank every deity I'd ever heard of that no one followed us. There was no more fight left in me if they had.

EIGHT

Mirraya had changed into a torchcleft early, before either Cala or Slapgren were awake. Winter was in the air, such as it was on the inhospitable Rameeka Blue Green. She flew to a tall mountain that overlooked the plains Cala had settled on. She sat on a rocky crag suspended over a vast glacier. It was bitterly cold up there that morning. A north wind hurled ice dust, having the effect of a frigid sandblaster. Mirri wanted to be alone. She wanted to be cold. Mirri needed to be very cold and very alone.

For many months she'd labored under the ever-increasing weight of Cala's yoke. The brindas was a kind female, even motherly at times, but she was a harsh taskmaster. Cala maintained that if she wasn't firm, none of her pupils would ever have learned enough to survive the trials they were to face. But Mirraya did not want to face trials. She did not wish to survive them if they were inevitable. What she wanted was to be the pretty, blossoming woman she had been when she had lived with her family before the Adamant destroyed everything.

No one, not even Uncle Jon, had explained to her why that awful empire had done such a horrific, unthinkable act of genocide. The Deft were a threat to no one. All the race had ever wanted was to be left alone. As shapeshifters, they were feared and envied, so they'd learned that isolation was their best friend. But the Adamant went out of their way not only to conquer them, but also made it their mission to delete them. Why? Mirraya knew for a fact her people hadn't hurt, offended, or challenged any other inhabitant of the galaxy.

Madness. It was all madness, and one she did not want to participate in. She decided she would perch on that crag until the cold slowly took her. Torchclefts were perfectly unsuited for an arctic environment. It wouldn't take long. After she was gone, Cala could do whatever she wanted. She could be the wise old hermit, claiming mighty power but accomplishing nothing. And Slapgren would be better off without Mirri, too. Sooner or later they'd be forced into hollon by their know-it-all teacher. Mirri would spare him the violation and humiliation of their melding just to please an old woman's sick desires.

Mirraya would always miss Uncle Jon. He saved her when it had been impossible. His love was the most intense she'd ever experienced. Her parents *had* to love her. Her relatives were *expected* to love her. But Uncle Jon *chose* to, for whatever reason. She giggled in her head. He wouldn't save her this time. He didn't know where she was or what she was about to allow to happen. Even if he did, the big-mouthed golden dragon would chirp and bluster at him until long after she was an ice cube. She would miss Uncle Jon.

Yes, she had to admit it, she'd miss Slapgren, too, that lunkhead. He was insensitive, crashing his way through life, but he had his good qualities, also. None came to mind as she sat there freezing to death, but she recalled noting some in the past. It was the cold. It was affecting her brain. Slapgren was loyal. Yes, that was one of his strong points.

She shook her head to clear it, then wondered why she cared? Wouldn't it be better to slip away addled than sharp as a new knife blade? Mirri knew the end was near. She began hallucinating. She smelled smoke whipping past her high on that windy peak. Only a dragon could start a fire …

Mirri turned slowly. Cala was nursing a bonfire, and Slapgren was just dropping a large load of wood on it from above. The flames curled way up into the sky, like they were directional signals to heaven. What an odd hallucination. It was so specific, so detailed. The smoke, the movement.

"If you don't come warm yourself now, child," shouted Cala, "I'll be forced to drag you over kicking and screaming."

Mirraya concluded numbly it was not a hallucination. They could never be so annoying.

"Leave me alone. You don't own me," she said very softly.

"No one does. But we can't just let you freeze."

"I can look out for myself."

"And look how well you've done so far," replied Cala, as she kicked at the wood.

"Leave me alone, I want to die."

"I assumed as much. But I cannot allow that."

"Why, because you're not done torturing me?"

"I'm not done *teaching* you yet. If I were torturing you, you'd know it well."

"Are you sure you should tease her?" asked Slapgren very quietly. "I mean, she seems kind of upset, sort of on the edge."

"Of course, she's upset and on the edge. She's a teenage girl. No matter what I say, she'll be one for a few more years. Hopefully, we'll all survive emotionally."

"Is it okay if I go talk to her?"

"No, because she's coming here before she turns into an ice sculpture. Then you can chat until your heart's content."

"Do you think she'll listen to me, about not hurting herself, I mean?"

"Sure. You're her future hollon mate. She'll have to."

Slapgren winced. "Could you stop saying that? It only pisses her off more and creeps me out."

"Fine. And I'll stop saying the sun will rise tomorrow and fish poop in the water. I'll stop saying everything that is completely obvious. Then you won't be creeped out. I can't have *that* on my conscience." She shivered. "Wait here while I retrieve the girl."

"Do you need my help?" He wished he hadn't asked the instant the words left his mouth.

"Have I ever?"

Slapgren let it drop.

Within five minutes Mirri had begun to thaw. Cala flew off to get more wood. Slapgren put a wing around Mirraya.

"I don't know what I'd have done if I lost you," he said, looking into the flames.

"You'd have done just fine." Then she winked at him. "You'd do better because you'd get my share of the agatcha."

"Don't joke about that. I'm serious. You and UJ are the only people I've got left in this whole big universe of indifference and malice."

"Wow," she said with a crooked smile, "when did you learn to talk so well?"

"What?" he said pulling back a bit.

"Really, you're starting to sound like Uncle Jon with your *indifference* and *malice*."

"I will choose to take that as a compliment."

"It certainly is," she said, snuggling closer to him under his wing. That caused him to recoil a little more.

"I'm so frustrated. I can't *stand* my life. I can't imagine *standing* my future."

"We'll get through this," he responded, trying to believe his own words.

"Sure, in like *twenty* years we may get a three-day pass to leave this prison. Oh boy."

"I'm going through this, too, you know? Lost my family, stuck here with you and Cala."

"Thanks for the encouragement and *support*. Have you ever considered being a crisis counselor?" She jerked her shoulder away from his light hold.

"I didn't mean *that*. Come on. I mean I'm stuck here just like you, and my life sucks just as much."

"Well I guess you var-tey are just tougher than us little girls, so you don't mind it."

Slapgren's wings dropped to the ground. He looked down and said nothing.

"Sorry. That was mean," she said quickly. "You're family, and I shouldn't attack family. Plus, you're all right. You're one of my two friends." She smiled. "You forgive me?"

He sat straight and looked serious. "Only if you don't kill yourself. If you do, I'm coming after you and giving you a spanking."

"Oh, you *are*, are you? And just how do you propose to do that?"

"We var-tey have our secrets."

"Like those silent farts of yours?"

He rolled his head back and forth. "A lesser gift, but yes."

She snuggled back up to him, although she no longer felt cold.

NINE

"The odds against your success were astronomical in the first place, Captain," said Al.

"Odds or no odds, I failed. That's all I know. The emperor is still on this side of the veil."

"I say you are entitled to quit. You tried twice, once at great personal risk, to assassinate the emperor. Let it go," responded Al.

"I gave my word."

"To your *sworn* enemy. That is not very binding."

"Yeah, but Harhoff's right. Killing off that bozo will probably topple the whole corrupt empire. Ultimately, that's *my* goal, too."

"Or it is simply one Adamant's *personal* goal, and it will do no such thing globally."

I shrugged. "Possible, but it's not like I have a better plan of my own."

"Repeatedly attempting the impossible will likely as not get you killed. Then think of the needless sacrifice I'd have made guarding you all those years," Al said.

Not on my watch. He was going to pay for that gab. "But, buddy, you can't think like that. *Stingray*, are you there?"

She was surprised to be called on, but responded, "Yes, Form. Where else might I be?"

"Lost in thought?" I replied.

"That is an idiom, not an actual location."

"Anyway, If I died, do you think Al would have wasted his time waiting by my side all those years?"

I could hear his *oh shit,* even though it was silent electronic pulses.

"I don't think he would have," she responded. "But I guess I can't speak for him. He did just say he'd have thrown those years down the sanitary unit."

"Generally, we say *toilet* in that expression," I corrected.

"But it isn't one. It's a—"

"I know, but it's more graphic that way."

"Husband, do you regret having waited to meet me?" she asked him evenly.

I was in *hog* heaven.

"Don't be ridiculous," he replied. "I love you."

"Oh, now I'm *ridiculous,* too? What, next I'm fat and you'll be looking at other computers who're newer models with bigger busses than I have?"

"No, sweetest, he's just trying to cause trouble. Have you forgotten he's like that? Please ignore him. I like your busses just like they are. I don't even want you to get bigger ones installed."

"Ridiculous, fat, old, no longer attractive, tiny busses, and *now* forgetful. I must be quite a disappointment for you, *Alvin.* I'm completely sorry for the harsh burden I've placed around your neck."

"Life of my love, the man is the devil. He's twisting my words and attempting to drive a wedge between us."

"Really? You think I'm that naive and stupid? He's only said a handful of words and none of them even remotely derogatory toward me."

"He's just that good at his game, heart of sweetness."

"Or maybe it slipped out from your subconscious right into your audio simulators?"

"I don't *have* a subconscious, lovimost. One was never programmed into me. You can ask the pilot. He'll tell you."

"So, I should share our private marital disputes with a perfect stranger now?"

"But, honey-bubble, he's listening all the time. He's heard every word we've said."

"That seals it. You let your voyeuristic chum eavesdrop on our innermost lives. What, did you lose a bet at cards interplay?"

"You mean *gambling*, pushy-gooshy?"

"And then he insults me by correcting me, yet again. If we weren't in the Wesleyan galaxy one and a half *billion* light-years from our own, I'd go home to mother."

"But, you don't ha ... it was my *impression* the Deavoriath didn't use mothers and fathers when constructing you. I will, however, be the first to admit I don't know how they fabricated a unit like you."

Man, I was starting to feel sorry for Al. He was digging his grave so quickly and so deeply it was painful. What a rookie. I was halfway thinking of jumping in on his defense. Then I remembered I had some internal sensors to recalibrate, so I didn't. Plus, theirs was a *couples* issue, not a matter for a perfect *stranger* to kibitz on. I was nothing if not the model of discretion.

It took three days for me to be certain the Als were once again speaking. They had internal connections they could have been using without me knowing, but I'm thinking those were down for repairs, too. Call me a stinker, but I loved every silent moment. Over the millennia, Al and I had each gotten and given a lot of guff, but I think I could safely declare myself the reigning champion. Hey, I didn't put one of those self-torpedoing words in his mouth. I only set him up. He only had himself to blame. Mostly.

As their mindless love chatter returned, so did my rumination about how I was going to do in the emperor. The internal security on his ship would be beyond impenetrable now. A direct assault with *Stingray* would be suicidal. Even if he had planned to be in public, which he hadn't, all outside engagements would be canceled for sure. How was I going to reach him? Simple. I wasn't, at least not anytime soon. I could wait for him to die of natural causes and claim credit, but who knew how long that might take? Plus, I doubted I'd be able to sell Harhoff on the notion I had anything to do with the fellow's demise.

As I was stuck in a rut, I reviewed my other options. I could drop in on my kids, but Cala made it abundantly clear that I was not welcome to "drop in on a whim and disrupt their already delayed training," as she put it.

For absolutely no reason in the universe, I could return to Peg's. That thought didn't even appeal to me and I'd recreated the joint. Azsuram? Why bother? The Adamant swarmed over every solid surface like fire ants on steroids. Sapale? Again, why bother? She blew me off definitively and with finality. EJ? I could try to hunt him down, but why? There was a chance I'd never see him again. He lost interest in me the moment I lost the Deft. Sure, he'd love to kill me slowly and painfully, but I didn't think he'd expend much time on the project.

I could continue my search for human descendants, but that was hardly a critical matter. They had two billion years to spread and evolve, so they weren't going anywhere fast. I had plenty of time to track them down later.

Maybe I could get a regular job, buy a little house in the suburbs, and start the search for a loving life partner? Oh, wait, I'd rather die a thousand times over. Plus, my low sperm sensor said it would be unfair to my life partner to saddle her with the prospects of an infertile mate.

I needed a way to get at Bestiormax. That was my only short-term concern, and there was no way around that fact. As I sat there frustrated and annoyed, Garustfulous came into the room to further frustrate and annoy me.

"Good morning, Captain Ryan," he veritably sang. "How are we this fine day?"

"Remind me to change the poison I'm putting in your food. This one seems to be making you cheerful."

He wagged a claw at me. "Always the jester. That's one of the things I've always loved about you, Ryan."

I spun to look at him. "You mean to tell me there exists personal qualities I possess that you *love*?"

"Yes. Many, in fact."

"I need a lifestyle change, and fast. I've strayed from the proper path."

He pointed at me again and smiled. "*Bozo.*"

"Huh?"

"You know, you're right, and I agree with you. *Bozo.*"

I twisted up my face. "You mean *bingo*?"

He tapped a claw to his muzzle. "Perhaps I do. Ah well. You look steeped in thought. May I help?"

"No."

"Take a moment to consider my offer. I'm a brilliant strategist with an agile intellect."

"No."

"All the time you need. I'm under no time pressure presently."

"No."

"Well, I'll give you a while to think over my words. I'll be in my cabin if you need me."

"Never. Please die."

He began whistling as he ambled away. Who'd have thought dogs would whistle one day? It struck me that if Garustfulous wanted to assassinate the emperor, he might just be able to pull it off. Of course, he wouldn't. They were like brothers. Too bad. The puke could finally be of some use to ...

No. I couldn't do *that*. No. I wasn't possibly *that* hard-hearted or cruel. No. It was too dark, too inhumane even for *me*. But I knew I'd lost enough of my soul to do it, to at least try? For the first time in forever, I scared myself with my thoughts. Could I step *that* far from the light?

TEN

I sat staring out a view screen at the globular cluster. It was at once spectacular and horrific. The visual of the myriad of stars shining was stunning. The knowledge that evil incarnate lived within its boundaries nearly melted my brain. If I still had a heart, it would have stopped beating. If I still breathed, I'd be suffocating. I sat there for days, staring. Was I going to do this? Was I capable of such a betrayal on such a scale? And if I could pay the price that would surely be asked, was I capable of paying it? How could I be? For two billion years, I was a force of good. I risked my life to help others so often I had come to assume it was my nature. But a good person could not be sitting in *that* vortex staring down at *that* globular cluster with *that* thought in his mind. I doubted even Evil Jon could conceive of the plan, let alone condone it. He couldn't be so indifferent as to imagine the benefits justified the risk. Because what I risked was the abandonment of any last shred of humanity I had left.

But the entire time I sat there pissing and moaning, I knew the deed was already done. The die was long since cast.

Of course, I was going to do it and of course I was going to pay the asking price. It was a done deal. The only thing that stopped me from giving the final order to land was the astonishment I felt knowing I *was* going to do what I was *about* to do.

"*Stingray*, land us near the acid pool on the planet down there where the dude with the mean voice lives." I issued the order matter-of-factly.

"Captain, I think that is unwise. No, wait, let me rephrase. That move is far too dangerous. I cannot condone it," said Al firmly.

"Well, lucky for me I don't need your approval to issue an order."

"Captain, I'm certain you have your reasons. But it is insane to do so no matter what you hope to achieve. The spirit that resides there is the very nexus of evil. I know you remember what he did to *Blessing*. Jon, I can't allow that to happen again. Please reconsider."

"Al, this is not the time to defy me. I must kill the emperor. I have tried everything I can think of. I have only one option, and it involves that life force."

"You do not *have* to kill the emperor. You *want* to, but what exactly depends on you doing so? Yes, you promised Harhoff you would. But two points. One, I doubt he believed you could do it in the first place, so his request has a shaky foundation. Two, you tried hard. I bet he'd release you from your commitment if you were to ask him."

"It's not just my promise. I know I'm not totally bound to do it because of that. But, Al, you and I, we've seen a lot, done a lot. These puppies, they gotta go. They are a cancerous infection spreading throughout this great galaxy. I want to stop them because they need stopping. I also owe them on behalf of all the individuals they've wronged. They have an enormous bar tab to pay, and I'm collecting it. It's what I do. That's what *we* do."

"And we will find a way. Jon, we're immortal. We have lots of time. There's no need to rush into something even if it were to speed the Adamant's demise."

"How many more people have to die? How many more species must vanish under their abuse? No. The longer we take to end their reign of terror, the worse it will be for the innocents." I sat up straight. "Al, realistically, what's the worst that can happen?" All the life was gone from my voice.

"I don't know if you mean that rhetorically or not, but I'll answer nonetheless. The worst that can happen is immeasurably bad."

"No, Al, my friend, it is not. The worst that happens is that three very old souls pass on from this existence. Maybe we do so in a blaze of glory. Maybe we do so suffering immense torment. But, in the end, the worst thing that happens is we three die. That, I submit, is a small price to pay if the Adamant can be stopped."

"I'm not comfortable with you speaking for *Blessing* in this case. Me, I'm bound to you until the end. I'm happy to march through the gates of hell with you if that's what it takes. But *Blessing*, well, this is not her fight."

"But you are happy with *you* speaking for her?"

"No." He hesitated. "Crap, you have a good point there, don't you?"

"Why, Al. In two billion years, I don't believe you've ever used the word *crap*."

"Desperate times, desperate measures. Plus, you're rubbing off on me like an oozing rash."

"Thanks, I think."

"*Blessing*," he said aloud, "what are your feelings? Is it wrong of the captain to take you back to that awful planet?"

"I've given this a lot of thought—nearly twenty picoseconds."

"That is a lot, my love," marveled Al.

"I knew such an action was likely when the Form brought us here. My choice is to stay with my man. My *men*, the both of you. If you're going down, I'm going down."

"Are you certain?" asked Al.

"Yes. No reservations. Plus, I must tell you I think the evil spirit is quaking in his boots knowing Jon Ryan is back. He's more afraid of us than we are of him."

"That would be a *whole* lotta afraid," I said with a whistle.

"I'm counting on it," she replied. If *Stingray* had lips, they'd be smiling.

"And what about Garustfulous?" asked Al. "Does he get a vote?"

"No. He's a POW and morally bankrupt. He gets a share of whatever bad befalls us. That's why I've had you drug him these last few days. I don't want to hear him try and wriggle his way out of what's coming."

"And for this, we both thank you," responded Al. "So, what is your plan?"

"If you knew the specifics, I don't think you'd rest any easier at night."

"It's a Jon Plan, then?"

"Of the highest, which means lowest, order," I replied.

"I can't wait to see it unfold," he said.

"You will be surprised. That much I can promise."

"Wouldn't have it any other way," he said. "We're commencing landing procedures now. I'll alert you when we're safely landed."

Safe in the land of evil incarnate. That was an oxymoron if I'd ever heard one. After touchdown, I headed out. I checked on Garustfulous first. He was out like a light bulb, drooling on this pillow. I walked directly toward the horrible acid pit. Where better to find my old pal?

As I entered the clearing, his voice came from everywhere. It was warm and welcoming. Gave me the goosebumps. "As I neither live nor breathe, if it isn't Jon Ryan. You are about the last soul I'd have expected to encounter today. How are you?"

"Well as can be expected, I suppose. You?"

"Unchanged throughout all time."

"I hope that's a good thing. I mean, if you felt like rat diarrhea forever, that'd kind of suck."

"Your concerns are duly noted, my friend. What is it that brings the one man to vanquish me back? Round two?"

"No. I'd never push my luck that hard."

"Oh, I bet you would."

"When I hear the word "bet" come out of your whatever, I get a little nervous."

"As well you should. So, if you are not here to test my powers again, what is it that brings you and your crew to such a dubious destination?"

"Sorry, I have to ask. Do you know already? I'm just curious."

"Jon, Jon. Information is a commodity, and no commodity is free. What would you pay me to know the truth of it?"

"A nice compliment?"

"Such a clever boy. I could use a servant like you. A position is open if you ever become interested."

"Not hardly, but thanks just the same." I rubbed my scalp. "Look, I came to ask for your help."

"No problem. Let me grab my coat, and we'll be off."

"Ah, just like that?"

"What did you expect?"

"Tough negotiations, impossible choices, and harsh compromises."

"Then you came prepared. What are you willing to pay?"

"You haven't heard what help I'm soliciting."

"If your maximum limit is below my minimum charge, there's no need to know, is there?"

"You've done this before?"

"You have to know I have."

"You ever make a deal you regretted or felt cheated by at the end?"

"Information, Jon. Again, you ask for something free."

"I want to end the Adamant Empire. Specifically, I want to assassinate the current emperor."

"That's not the price you're willing to pay, you old robot. That's the mission. You're hoping to lower my price by dangling an alluring prospect before my eyes."

"Maybe."

"Yes. I will warn you. It won't work, can't work. Do you know why?"

"Not a single clue."

"Because the only cause I'm committed to is me. The only institution I wish to see happy and improved is, again, me. The Adamant are cruel masters. There have been worse. I'm confident there will be others just as bad. They are all the same: nothing to me."

"Oh well, can't blame me for trying."

"But I can. You see, in testing my patience, you run a far greater risk than you can know. The price, Jon. What will you lose?"

"Myself."

"Really? I was certain you were going to offer that overgrown dog asleep on your ship."

"Would that have been enough?"

"Not by the length of the universe. He's so insignificant it boggles the mind."

"Figured as much."

"But, really, Jon. You offer yourself? What kind of prisoner would you be if I knew you could defeat me at any time? It would be like a sheep laying claim to a panther."

"Me without the membrane generator."

"Or the magic cube?"

"No vortex either."

"That's a very tempting offer. But, as you might guess, I'm short on trust and long on crafting an unbreakable pact. Let me read your offer back to you. If I help you—"

I raised a finger. "*Successfully* help me. If we don't win, I don't owe."

"Clever boy, yet again. Fine, if I aid you in your quest to kill the current Adamant emperor and we succeed, you will surrender yourself to me for all eternity after removing your force field generator and abandoning your vortex?"

"Something like that."

"Do not test me, *human*," he thundered. "A flippant remark like that might be your last. State your offer without generalities."

"If we kill Bestiormax and escape, I will give you me, me minus a shield generator or a cube. I will do so within a year after we assassinate the emperor. There are matters I must attend to before I return here with my payment."

"Done."

I knew at once it was.

"You know how badly I want you, Jon?"

"So badly you let me slip in that year-long delay."

"I was being superficial before, Jon, but I must say, you are the clever one."

"Thanks."

"So, what is your plan? I swoop in and vaporize the emperor?"

"Really? You think I'd come up with a simple plan like that?"

"No, honestly, I'd hoped for more."

"The operation involves you leaving this nurturing globular cluster. I don't want to overtax you. How long can you remain, you know, viable when you're not here?"

"Information, Jon."

"No, I need to know to plan the timing."

"A month, maybe. The longer I'm away, the weaker I get. But, to prevent you tricking me into dissipating, at some point I must break and leave, no matter what the level of progress might be."

"I will—"

"I know, transport me both directions. I've heard that one before. My trust has never run that deep, nor shall it."

"So, if you bail on me, the deal is off."

"Jon, we have already struck the deal. It cannot be unilaterally altered."

"But you hadn't stated all your conditions."

"Imagine if you will, me, however you picture me. Now add me patting myself on the chest. I'm saying *evil incarnate*."

"Which I knew coming into this."

"Which concerns me all that much more. When a clever boy like you overlooks details in a contract, I wonder what *I'm* missing.

"Excellent. If I have given you pause, so much the better."

"Be snug now, my friend. Remember the mine-for-eternity clause. I will get my suffering back with interest."

As cold as the grave, I responded. "I'm kind of counting on it. Climb aboard."

ELEVEN

"Monitor, I have an incoming ship requesting to dock," said the transport tech as he stared intently at his screen.

Monitor Benfinitas paced over to look. "Are they scheduled to arrive?"

"No, sir."

"Then refuse their approach. Inform the Dark Guard of their attempt, and fire on them if they continue in this direction. No unauthorized vessels may approach *Excess of Nothing* under any circumstances. Not with all the threats His Imperial Lord faces."

"I think this might constitute an exception, sir."

Benfinitas slapped the back of technician Malorate's head soundly. "What part of *no exceptions* do you not understand?"

"The ones concerning His Imperial Lord's family. You know how touchy he is about them," replied Malorate, rubbing his wounded pelt.

"What are you blathering about? What family?"

"It is Wedge Leader Garustfulous himself who is hailing us."

"That's preposterous. Garustfulous is dead."

"Beg pardon, sir, he's MIA, not on the dead scroll."

Benfinitas shoved Malorate's chest with his flank. "Move over. I'll get to the bottom of this."

"This is Monitor Benfinitas of the *Excess of Nothing*. Identify yourself."

"I did, worm bait. Allow us to dock or I shall suck out what little brains you possess through your eye socket."

"You claim to be His Imperial Lord's cousin. Can you prove it?"

"Yes. It's complicated, so you'll need to listen carefully and take notes. You look at me. You realize who I am. You allow me to dock. Any questions?"

"Pl ... please submit a current bioscan."

A second later, Garustfulous said flatly, "Done."

"This does appear in order," said Benfinitas mostly to himself.

"I feel so much better knowing I am me. Now unshield a dock."

"A-99-A-35, sir. I'll inform His Imperial Lord of your arrival," responded Benfinitas.

"Understood. Oh, and Monitor Benfinitas?"

"Yes?"

"If you feel you have some place you may safely hide, I suggest you go there now."

Benfinitas did not acknowledge that last remark. He did feel the boring eyes of all the monitor-hub personnel searing his back, however.

"Wedgelet Lolirp, I need to use the restroom. You're in command while I'm away."

"Sir."

A small detail of honor guard flanked the hatch as it opened. Garustfulous strode past them like they were invisible. He held a blaster to Jon Ryan's back, marching the prisoner in front of himself. Behind Garustfulous followed Group Captain Harhoff. He carried a small suitcase. The trio proceeded without asking for directions, and the detail fell in behind them, trying to keep up the quick pace. The officer of the watch started to greet Garustfulous, but refrained at the last moment. He correctly surmised the look on Garustfulous's face was brooding and uninviting.

When the three travelers arrived at the doors to the Imperial section, they were confronted and stopped by five Midriacks. The fact that the five were stationed *outside* the private residence attested to the heightened security instituted since Jon's last visit.

"State your business," hissed the lead Midriack. He held his staff up between Garustfulous and himself.

Garustfulous swept a glance of the guard from toe to head. "None. I have no business with my cousin. Step aside."

The guard thumped Garustfulous in the chest to halt his attempt to brush past.

"How *dare* you. Your entire clan will suffer for this affront," snapped Garustfulous.

"Protocols have *evolved* since your vacation began. You will submit to bioscan, and I will smell your fur."

"I just had one."

"And you will have another or die where you stand."

"Oh, very well. But be quick about it. My friend and I are anxious to present this prisoner to my cousin."

"Then, unfortunately, your friend and you will suffer a grievous disappointment. Neither this unauthorized officer nor this unwashed scum will pass my pod while one still lives."

"That is not your decision to make, hollow bones. I am *kin*. I will *do* as I see fit."

The guard said nothing by way of response.

A medtech approached Garustfulous gingerly and performed the scan. "He is who he says he is," the man said nervously.

"And who is that?" asked the guard.

"Garustfulous."

The guard leaned in and pressed his nose against Garustfulous's cheek. "Yes, I concur. And no fear. I'm impressed, cousin of my master."

"Then you'll allow my friend and prisoner to pass without my killing you and your pets. For as surely as I have no fear of you, I will take no orders from you."

"Then we will have a bloody fight here in the passage, shan't we?" said the guard powering up his staff. The other four flashed theirs to life.

"I would ask you a question first," said Garustfulous to the lead. "Would you prefer to lose *one* of your kinsman in battle or *four* of them?"

"I don't do riddles," was his terse response.

"Answer the question."

"One, of course."

"Of these four sad excuses for warriors, which do you secretly dislike the most? Hmm? Which would you rather see die in pain, prevented from achieving your notion of perfection in the afterlife?"

"None. I have no preferences. They are all kin."

Garustfulous leaned in under the guard's hood and pressed his lips to his ear. "Come, friend, I'm offering you a choice. Surely there is one you trust the least, one you fear the most. Whisper his name to me. You will thank yourself in an instant." Garustfulous stepped back to where he was before.

Garustfulous turned to the four guards. "Which of you goes by the name of Garttelass?"

The furthest figure raised his staff a centimeter. Then his chest exploded silently. His purple blood shot out in an expanding donut shape until it struck something hard. A wall, a face, or the lead guards cowl.

The guard who'd spoken the name Garttelass bowed deeply and stepped aside to allow the three guests inside.

The trio entered as if nothing grotesque and inexplicable had just happened. Garustfulous went directly to his cousin's personal suites. There, the Midriack on duty made no attempt to block his advance. The door opened automatically, and he led the party in.

Bestiormax walked quickly toward his beloved cousin. "Garut, when we thought you were dead, it saddened our heart." He extended his paw holding the ring of office so Garustfulous might kiss it."

"No thanks," Garustfulous said pushing the paw down. "I've already eaten."

The emperor looked at his kinsman with unbridled horror. Then, he broke out laughing. "You were always getting it over on me, weren't you, you old hound? You've never changed."

"Oh, if you only knew the millionth of it."

Upon hearing that, Bestiormax had a puzzled look on his face, but he let it pass. "Come, sit. We have food and drink a'plenty. Bitches at our beck and call. Life, my cousin, is good here."

"Thank you, old friend," he responded.

All three sat, though Jon made it a point to do so awkwardly, as he was acting the part of prisoner. The emperor sat at the head of the low table. His Midriack guards fanned out to have a clear line of sight on each guest.

"So, who is this officer you bring that we do not know?" asked Bestiormax.

"This is my partner in crime Group Captain Harhoff. He currently serves aboard *Rush to Glory*." Garustfulous took a big swallow of the ale he'd been poured. "Ah, that's something I've not experienced in much too long."

The ever more puzzled emperor asked, "What, had such fine ale?"

"No. Eaten or drunk anything. Odd feeling, but not altogether unpleasant."

"My," said Bestiormax as he had no idea what else to say. "Well there's an endless supply. Help yourself. You, too, Group Captain. Any friend of our cousin's is a friend of this court."

"Oh, he's not my *friend*. I said he was my partner in *crime*. No, I could never be this one's friend. He's a visionary you see. He believes in causes larger than himself. He's willing to sacrifice mightily to achieve a noble goal. He's not piss-worthy in my book."

"Whatever crime is he partners in with you. Oh my, did that come out sounding sober?"

Garustfulous smiled wickedly. "A minor one of no long-term consequence, I promise you."

"Ah. I'm certain that's a good thing."

"You mean *we*," corrected Garustfulous.

"We? We what?"

"You said *I'm certain*. You likely meant *we're certain*."

"Yes. How odd a slip. Ah well, it's no doubt your company that reminds m ... us of simpler times."

Garustfulous belched.

"And this hideous appearing prisoner, who might he be?"

"Well, he might be Elvis or the Easter Bunny, but he's not. This," he poked Jon's shoulder, "is the fly in your royal

91

ointment, the pus in your pimple. This is the criminal Jon Ryan."

Three Midriack lunged toward Jon, and two moved to cover the emperor. For his part, Bestiormax nearly crawled over his guards to distance himself from Jon. Neither Jon nor Garustfulous as much as flinched. The guards stopped short of impaling the prisoner. His Imperial Lord cautiously returned to his seat, his eyes never leaving the prisoner.

"How can you be *certain* we are safe? This criminal is resourceful and cruel," asked Bestiormax.

"He's not actively involved in this dog and pony show. He's just window dressing."

"We say, cousin, your disappearance seems to have affected your nerves in a negative manner. We hardly know you."

The three Midriack closest to the guests ignited their staffs.

"Oh, you know me, Bestiormax. *And I looked, and behold a pale horse: and his name that sat on him was Death, and Hell followed with him. And power was given unto them over the fourth part of the earth, to kill with sword.*"

"*Kill* them!" screamed Bestiormax like a little girl. "Kill them *all.*"

None of the guards moved. They were frozen as if statues in a park during winter. Bestiormax shot his eyes wildly around the room. The functionaries and other guests were equally still.

"What's ... what's the meaning of this?" howled Bestiormax in a panic.

"As I suggested, cousin, it means Death has come, Hell a'following, with a sword to take your head."

"Th ... this joke has gone much too far. Cease now, and *all* will be forgiven."

"If by a joke you mean your pitiful reign and meaningless empire, then I agree with you. As to forgiveness, well, that's not my thing. I'm more the opposite, the reaper of souls, so to speak." He nodded to Harhoff, who had been tasked with the actual assassination.

The group captain moved quickly toward his soon-to-be late emperor.

"*No*," screamed Bestiormax. "We forbi—"

Presumably, the once ruler of all he surveyed was going to say forbid it, but that would never be known. Harhoff produced a large, angry-looking dagger from his waist and roughly sawed through Bestiormax's neck. He picked up the bleeding head and dropped it in the suitcase he'd brought precisely for that purpose.

"I hate to eat and run, but I really think it's best we be moving on," said evil incarnate to the decapitated body of the emperor. "No hard feelings, eh?"

The embodiment of evil received no reply, obviously.

With the room still full of motionless figures, the three travelers walked casually out of the private suites, out the massive doors of the imperial sector, and back to the stolen shuttle that had ferried them from *Blessing*. Harhoff had his proof that the reign of the Imperial Lord Emperor Bestiormax-Jacktus-Swillyforth-Anp was over, as was the rule of his house. Jon had fulfilled his promise and owned the knowledge that the accursed empire of the Adamant had started to fall. Evil? Well, evil had his man, who happened to be a robot.

TWELVE

Because we were sick bastards, Harhoff and I were really looking forward to the moment. To savor it most securely, we decided to insist it happen while we were still aboard *Stingray*, drifting in the middle of the galactic void. The evil voice, the one that said I should call him Ralph, was still in possession of Garustfulous. Before we returned to his home and to the source of his power, we wanted to see Garustfulous's response when he was released. To do so on his own turf risked giving Ralph an unfair advantage. Better safe than sorry.

"Okay, Ralph, release him," I said, almost giggling.

"Where is it you fancy I should wait?" he replied. "Shall I float disembodied in the air like a ghost?"

"Couldn't care less," I responded. "Just get out of his body so ... so I can determine that he's unharmed."

"Yes, we don't want any negative consequence to befall our friend," said Harhoff. I believe those were his first words to Ralph. For some reason, he was intimidated by the malevolent beast.

"This is not my first rodeo, boys," replied Ralph. "This

worthless wretch, who by the way is no one's friend, will be fine. May we return to my home now?"

"As neither of us wrote this into the contract, I'm going to have to insist you obey the captain of this vessel," I said, not knowing if those were wise words or not.

"Oh, very *well*. You know you're a pair of juvenile delinquents, don't you?"

Garustfulous collapsed to the deck like a wet towel.

From all around us, we heard, "There, are you happy?"

"That's a rather open-ended question, but no. I hope to be one day, so thanks for your concern," I spouted back.

"Look, he's moving," yelped Harhoff as he pointed to the floor.

"Oh, my head," moaned Garustfulous. "Did anybody get the ID on the bus that hit me?"

"He's fine, just a total wuss," said the dispersed Ralph.

"Who's a wuss?" whined Garustfulous.

"You, ya big wuss," I said as I grabbed his arm to help him to a chair. "Do you want a glass of water?"

"No thank you. I seem to be nauseated and confused." He shook himself like a wet dog. Then he looked around the room. "How did I get here? The last thing I recall was having dinner in my quarters. Now I'm seated here, and this officer is smiling at me like I'm a sideshow freak. Sir, who are you?"

"Group Captain Harhoff."

"Have we met before?"

"Depends on how one defines that, I suppose," he replied with an even bigger grin.

"That answer is unacceptable. However, I have a more pressing question. Why are you covered in blood? Why, for that matter, am *I* covered in blood? And why is the captain here," he gestured toward me, "clean as a Sunday suit?"

Harhoff's face winced. "Kind of a long story," he asked more than stated.

"Oh, here," boomed Ralph, "I'll fix this."

Garustfulous pretty much jumped out of his skin. Such a ubiquitous, evil voice was apparently among the last things he was prepared for. Then he froze and had an even blanker than usual look on his face.

"There," said Ralph, "I filled in the gaps."

In the old Bugs Bunny cartoons, when a character was getting really mad, they puffed up and expanded, steam whistling from their ears. That's kind of how Garustfulous looked. "You *used* me to assassinate my beloved cousin, childhood playmate, and sole link to promotion and wealth? You went light-years out of your way to find evil itself and shoved it in my ear? *How dare you* doesn't begin to cover my disgust, contempt, and sudden loss of viability in my career."

"What? I'm *certain* if you explain to your court-martial panel exactly what happened, they will believe you rather than the obvious facts," replied Harhoff with no semblance of sincerity.

"You're less funny than *him*," he spat, pointing at me. "I would not have thought such a thing possible."

"Are you certain you don't want to leave him with me?" asked Ralph. "He's quite the self-righteous prick, if you ask me. I'm quite good at handling that type, you know."

"Nah, I'd miss the scruffy bastard," I replied, messing up Garustfulous's hair.

"I will not have you making decisions on my behalf any longer," shouted Garustfulous.

"Ah, countryman, trust me on this. You do *not* want to linger on Ralph's world," said Harhoff quickly.

"Who the devil is *Ralph*?" howled Garustfulous.

"Exactly," I said. "Let's move on. Ralph, we will drop you

off in a couple minutes. Please don't try and pull any fast ones. I'm watching you." I did that two fingers to my eyes thing but was forced to toss it in several directions.

"Oh, there'll be no tricks. I have what I want and wouldn't risk it for all the souls in purgatory."

"Perfect."

"And, Jon, in case you think you can escape our little deal with distance, either in spacial distance or in time, that's not how it works. Precisely one year to the *second* after Harhoff parted Bestiormax's head from his body, you are mine. There can be no escape."

"No problem. Escape is not my plan."

"Why does that worry me so?" asked Ralph.

"Because you're a worry wart, Ralphie-pooh. Try to go with the flow a bit more. Life's short. Smell some black roses or something."

"Now I know you're up to something. Life is not short, at least not mine or yours. Please, tell me what I'm missing here," chided Ralph.

"*Information*, my good fellow, is never free. What are you willing to offer?" I asked, peppering in as much asshole intonation as I could.

"Are we there yet?" was Ralph's only response.

THIRTEEN

We dropped our evil incarnate associate off quickly and left even faster. Once we were millions of light-years away, Harhoff and I could relax. Garustfulous, not so much. He went on and on about our violation of his corporeal integrity, his powerful desire to maim and kill us, and his general disgust with the current state of social mores. He also showered so much and so often I wondered how his fur remained intact. I tried to convince him bathing was not going to help, unless he could turn himself inside out like a popcorn kernel, since Ralph was *internal*, not *external* to his being. He took surprisingly little solace from that reassurance. Go figure.

"Here," I said setting a glass of ale down in front of Harhoff, "a celebration is in order."

We toasted, and he took a sip. "This is simply marvelous. Where did you get such a superb ale? Don't tell me humans ever achieved this lofty height in the brewing sciences," he said, staring at the golden liquid.

"Nah, this is not at all like our ale, but it's serviceable. I stole it from Bestiormax. Hey, Little G, you want some ass-kicking beer?"

He hurried over. "Yes. It's possibly the only treatment that can cure me." He sat down and looked at me, well, like a dog anticipating his dinner.

"So, let me get this straight. You had the presence of mind to snatch a bottle of the emperor's ale as we left?"

"No," I said after swallowing a big gulp. "You crazy? We needed to book. No, I stuffed a few bottles down my pants while you were sawing his head off. By the way, that reminds me, you didn't bring a very sharp knife to the execution. Sloppy, dude."

"One, you're unbelievable. Two, I intentionally brought a serrated blade. A meat seller's knife would take too long to cut through the neck bones."

"Oh, so you're an expert in beheading, now are you?"

"May we change the subject?" moaned Garustfulous. "As poorly as I feel, you're making my condition worse with your gruesome dialogue. And keep the ale coming."

"Probably not a bad idea," I agreed. "So, now that the empire is down the toilet, what are your plans?"

"Let's not bury it until it's dead," replied Harhoff.

"Wait, I thought you said if we remove Bestiormax, the house of cards tumbles."

He bobbed his head side to side.

"Why am I not liking that *non* answer?"

"His removal was *necessary*, but not *sufficient* to ensure the empire collapses anytime soon."

"You seem to have omitted that amendment when first we spoke."

"I'd rather say I glazed over the particulars with an eye toward speedy communications. We were at risk of capture at any moment, if you'll recall."

"I do recall, but what I recall is we were slamming down musto in the quiet seclusion of your quarters."

"It doesn't matter now. We are where we are, tactically speaking."

"Which translates as?"

"There is still much work to be done."

"You know, if I had a temper, which naturally I don't, I think I'd unload on you right about now." I sat down my glass.

"Our work from this point forward is much simpler. Plus, many others can participate."

"Translation?"

"The empire is now critically unstable. But an unstable monolith will not tumble unless it is made to. We need to push it hard enough to cause it to crumble. That will require military strikes as well as political incursions."

"Let me guess. You want me to be the next emperor? Lord Ryan Dog the First."

"Probably unrealistic."

"You think? So, maybe you're assigning me extra credit homework from the military strike column?"

He shrugged. "It does match your species and qualification specifications."

"Wait," Garustfulous said. "You two are talking about open rebellion, high crimes and misdemeanors against my society." He whopped Harhoff's chest with the back of his paw. "Your society, too. I won't stand by idly while you plot to destroy everything I hold dear and sacred."

"First, Little G, keep in mind you may have warm fuzzy feelings toward all things Adamant. They, however, have holos of you leading the raiding party that assassinated the emperor. Second, you can lie to most folk, but not to me. You have no loyalty to any person, place, or thing except yourself. You hold nothing sacred but your wallet. The only thing dear to you is your safety."

He rolled his head a second. "Normally I'd take you to task for such insults. However, given the facts as they are and the situation as it is, I will, instead, agree that you are essentially correct."

"You can either join us, or you can risk it on your own," said Harhoff. "The fight ahead will be long, and it will be hard. I could use a person of your uniquely sociopathic tendencies. It's your decision."

"Wait," I interrupted. "Neither of you are going home. You two killed the emperor. Promotions and retirement are hardly in order."

Harhoff smiled knowingly. "He killed the emperor. I was aboard *Rush to Glory* the entire time. I have proof."

"That's not possible," protested Garustfulous. "There are images of you in our assault team."

"I'm in charge of security on *Rush to Glory*. Being a very clever fellow and holding that position, I can make anything appear to be true. I was careful to avoid any bioscans. There was an Adamant who chanced to look like me in your party, but it could *not* have been me." He patted his chest.

"But I had bioscans. Ralph told me."

"You did. But, again, as the clever and resourceful head of security that I am, I can create a new identity for you. You will be born again."

"You could do that? I mean, if he were ever bioscanned, wouldn't the records show him to be Garustfulous?" I asked.

"There is some risk, but I believe I can make it safe. His alternative is to disappear and never be found."

"In a galaxy teaming with Adamant," I added.

"Not an enviable position," replied Harhoff.

"Me, a rebel? A covert agent of destruction?" He shook his

head. "Sounds like a plan." He held up his glass and we all toasted.

I pointed to the suitcase on the floor beside Harhoff's paw. "Just how do you plan on using that disgusting artifact?"

"I will make images of it go viral. Irrefutable proof of his death will be everywhere. Even then there are likely to be official denials, with simulated holos of him offered as evidence to the contrary. But those inclined to believe he's dead will know it's true. The desperate supporters hoping to retain power know in the end that someone somewhere has his head."

"So, you return to your ship with your newborn crew mate. What about me?" I asked.

"You do what you have been doing, what you do best. You strike at the empire and help cause it to topple."

"There's just one of me. The empire is kind of big, you know." I held my hands way apart to indicate size.

"It *is* large. Others elsewhere will need to strike. But when a few key installations are destroyed, doubt and suspicion will drive a wedge between those who aspire to control the empire. The splintered oligarchy will kill itself off sooner rather than later."

"So, you already have a list of key installations in mind? Funny you didn't mention them *before* I signed on?" I snarked.

"In the interest of time—"

I held up a hand. "No need to complete the lie. Just hit me. What do you want taken out?"

"A handful of targets."

"Only a handful? That can't be too many. What, three?"

"If you remove three, we can talk."

I rolled my eyes. "You should have been a politician."

"Who says I'm not planning on it?"

"I *knew* there was something I didn't like about you. Thank you. I have you in perspective now."

"The most critical target is the armory planet of Plinius. All of the weapons that fuel the Adamant machine are manufactured and housed there."

Garustfulous had been drinking the last of his beer. He sprayed it when he heard those words. "You think it's even remotely possible to attack and destroy Plinius? It's better protected than *Excess of Nothing* is. Such a feat is unimaginable."

"Hence my assigning it to Jon," responded Harhoff flatly. "If anyone can, he can."

"But my point is that *no one* can. No ten advanced races combined could as much as crater the surface."

"This doesn't sound promising," I said.

"There's no great rush," replied Harhoff. "You can plan your attack for weeks, maybe as long as a month. I'm sure you'll come up with something."

"Is it too late to withdraw from our covert band?" I asked.

"Yes, it is."

"Then I wish to make it official. I hate you."

"That," said Harhoff with a grin, "I can live with."

FOURTEEN

Harhoff had a ship stashed in a charged gaseous nebula not too far from *Rush to Glory*. That way I could pick him up and drop him off in secret. As soon as we were done with the beer and the depressing news of my new mission, I dropped him and Garustfulous off. I was actually a little sad to see Harhoff go. He was a kindred spirit and a good egg. Garustfulous? Wow, I was so exited to take out that garbage I nearly danced a jig. But I hated jigs. Just a stupid sailor dance for stupid sailors. I've *never* been drunk enough that I ever danced one.

Alone again, I reviewed once more the information on Plinius. Doing so made me more and more depressed. The place wasn't a tight as Fort Knox. It was ten gazillion times tighter. The space above it had so many warships I was surprised they didn't continually collide with one another. The ground below consisted of megalopolises on large continents. Each big city was shielded with a high-energy barrier. Nothing in real space was getting through those. I could fold space past them, but once inside, I was confronted by certain death. It was like the proverbial dragon where, when you cut off one head, two magically appeared to replace it.

Sure, there were so many troops I could walk across the planet stepping on their heads and never touch the ground. Sure, the air was filled with warships of every kind and size. Sure, sensors occupied positively any otherwise unoccupied space, such as any rare, open terrain. But those weren't enough. No, there had to be countless drones flying and rolling over the entire planet. The sea had more floating and submarine drones than it did little fishes. If I sneezed anywhere on Plinius, thousands of well-armed, ill-intentioned soldiers would know about it and come a-calling before I could find a Kleenex. The planet was unassailable by sheer number of defensive measures. Ah, the Adamant, nothing if not given to overkill.

I briefly fantasized about asking Ralph for help again. But I quickly dismissed that one. Even he would be overmatched. Plus, old Ralphie wasn't really a team player *and* I had nothing more I was willing to barter.

"Als, have you two gone over the reports we have on Plinius?" I asked.

"Yes, Captain, we have. Quite a piece of work. It combines state-of-the-art manufacturing with paranoid security protocols. Truly amazing," replied Al.

"I wasn't asking for a critique. I want a plan to take it out."

"You realize, Form, you're asking for a way to destroy an entire planet? Even if you are only asking for a procedure that will lead to a sterile surface, such a task would be daunting," added *Stingray*.

"But not impossible, right?" I responded.

"Wrong," said Al. "I believe it is unwise to assume the single ship could "destroy" an entire planet, whatever one means by "destroy.""

"Well, I don't mean blow it up like you'd blow up a building. I just need to render it uninhabitable. That can't be so hard?"

"And you base that assumption on what? The intervention of *both* Santa Claus and your fairy godmother on your behalf?" That was, naturally, Al commenting.

"This is serious, Al. Can you be an adult for just a second?"

"I *am* serious. Captain, the asteroid that wiped out the dinosaurs is estimated to have transferred 4×10^{23} Joules of energy to the planet. That's equivalent to the energy delivered by two-hundred million good-sized nuclear weapons. To actually *explode* a planet the size of Plinius would take a bomb in the 10^{33} Joule range. But you can't just drop a 10^{33} Joule bomb on the planet from space. It would waste most of it's explosive force off into space. The energy output of your home star Sol is around 10^{27} Joules per second. Do you see where I'm going with this? You'd have to put ten *thousand* Sols in the center of Plinius for a second to blow it up."

"Ten to the thirty-third Joules, eh? I'll admit, that's a lot."

"That's so gracious of you to agree with facts, Pilot."

"Look, if we used the quantum decouplers at short range, that would produce a walloping amount of energy."

"Yes. And *if* we could ignite a goodly portion of Plinius at once, you are correct, we'd do her in," replied Al with a clear edge to his tone.

"Okay, let me do a quick mind experiment."

"This should be good," replied Al, either to himself or to *Stingray*, not sure which it was.

"The QU waves move at the speed of light. It would take a trivial amount of time to have them interact with a mass in the range we're talking about. So if I put enough QU deep in Plinius, they could theoretically trigger a mass explosion."

"I think you'd be better off contacting George Lucas and renting the Death Star. It would be much more realistic."

"That's not *helpful*, Al. Let's focus on reality."

"Fine. *When* shall we begin, because we have not yet."

"*Stingray*, how deep would I have to place how many QU to do the trick?" I was trying to cut out the snarky one.

"Oh, maybe one hundred QUs at ten to one hundred kilometers depth."

"Well that's doable."

"Yes."

"Yes *but*? I definitely heard a *but* there."

"I'm sorry, Form. I did not mean to imply I have a but. There is, however, the matter of how the QU waves could access contact with such a large solid mass simultaneously. If the planet were a gas giant, it might be possible. But Plinius is solid rock with a molten core."

"We *have* a solution. We're just talking details of that solution here," I said most unconvincingly.

"Pilot, the clearing up those details might just violate the laws of physics."

"*All* the laws of physics?" I asked halfheartedly.

"All of them in *this* universe," he responded triumphantly.

"You know what, Alvin? You're absolutely right," I replied.

"Why don't I like the sound of that response?"

"Because you're a festering hemorrhoid?"

"Aside from that."

"Don't you see? I just need to change the laws of physics."

"That's all?"

"Yeah, and only for a microsecond or two."

"Oh, then it should be child's play. By the time the universe notices we've broken its fundamental laws, we'll be long gone. It'll never catch us."

"We can only hope," I said with a wink. "Als, put us in a

cloaked orbit around Plinius. We need to gather some data before we can delete the planet."

"Sure," replied Al dubiously. "Orbit we can do. Delete the planet, well, that might just be another of your delusions leaking out of your head."

"Ye of little faith," I replied.

"We have *no* faith, but for our faith in the fact that you are about to make a fool of yourself. For the record, we're popping popcorn and getting front row seats. This will be good."

Once in concealed orbit around our target, I had the Als begin to do detailed geology surveys of the planet. We had surface maps and population data from Harhoff. But I needed a very accurate picture of the subsurface structure. For my plan to work, I needed to set off an explosion deep underground. The easiest way to dig really deep was to start digging really deep. Let nature do the heavy lifting. It was going to take a while even for the Als to compile the information. Plinius was large and we could only pulse open the membrane for an instant at a time to avoid detection. The place was literally swarming with Adamant. A good proportion of the land masses were covered with either factories or warehouses. The planet was one big production installation.

While they labored at the mapping, I ran various simulations in my head. I needed to release as much energy as far down as possible if I was to actually destroy the planet. The size of the explosion clearly needed to be massive, massively massive. Setting off QU waves or using exotic matter just didn't generate the levels of energy required to do the job. Even a colliding black hole down deep wouldn't do it. Not that I had a clue how to pull that off, but it wasn't enough. But I had a notion where I could release more than enough energy.

In fact, the problem I struggled with was limiting the explosion to just Plinius. Yeah. Big boom-boom.

Long ago, I faced an enemy called the Last Nightmare. They moved from universe to universe conquering and then eradicating all life in their new homes. They had a stronghold in a specific universe from which they attacked. I learned from my Deavoriath allies that universe hopping was not for the faint hearted. There existed an infinite number of parallel universes. Most had laws of physics very different from ours. In the case of the Last Nightmare, they were limited to destroying only universes with similar enough laws that permitted them to exist. If they tried to invade an incompatible space, there'd be an explosive annihilation. When we made the journey to their home universe, the Deavoriath went to great lengths to prove it would be safe for us to do so.

My sketchy plan was to open a portal between two incompatible universes deep under the surface of Plinius. While that was easy to draw on paper, the details were extremely tricky. As I mentioned, if I opened too large a rift, the volume of annihilation could be dangerously big. I was dealing with unknowns in a setting where a mistake could destroy major portions of my galaxy. Talk about throwing the baby out with the bath water. Killing everyone in a ten kiloparsec radius would be effective in eliminating the planet, but no one would be left to thank me for my efforts.

There was the issue of escape. With an explosion on such a scale, I needed to be sure we could get far away quickly if we hoped to avoid self-destruction. Al would never forgive me if I fried him and his new wife. It wasn't like I could set a timer on a bomb and leave. No. I had to be in *Stingray* to open a universe-to-universe rift. There was no spare vortex and even if there were, there was no one to pilot it. That was one reason

I was vague about my plan with Al. Once he learned of it, his disapproval meter was going to red line.

It took about a week to complete a detailed survey. I was pleased to learn the subsurface of Plinius was riddled with deep caves and pockets. None were quite far enough down to use in and of themselves, but they constituted good starting points for digging. I reasoned that a pocket, being an island of open space, was better to work in than a tunnel. If we were detected it would be hard to get to us if there was no easy access. Yes the Adamant had PEMTUs and their ships could theoretically materialize anywhere like we could. But, charging into a small opening in solid rock was not something one did lightly. Me, I chose to because I was desperate *and* insane. They were hopefully neither. Hopefully being a key word I hated to rely on when my death was the point in question. Then again, fighter pilot here.

"*Stingray*, do you have files on our war with the Last Nightmare?" I asked when I had all the information I needed.

"Why, yes, Form. That seems to me an odd request. Are you well?"

"Give the man some rope, dearest. He'll hang himself soon enough." Yeah, my pal Al there.

"Also, I need you to access ancient, I mean *more* ancient files having to do with Deavoriath conquests. Specifically, they cast an enemy species from our universe into an incompatible one. You got those, too?"

"Yes. Every vortex manipulator holds all the knowledge of the Deavoriath."

"So are you currently capable of performing such a feat?"

"Yes, it's—"

"*Freeze!*" commanded Al. "It just hit me where this is going and I forbid it. End of discussion."

Glad I knew that was coming. "Ah, Al, I think I should

110

introduce myself. I'm *General* Jon Ryan, captain of this vessel and commander of you. This is a critical military operation, not a friendly discussion. While I occasionally benefit from your input, I *never* require your permission. If you have a problem with any of that, I will switch you off. Now we've arrived at the *end of discussion*."

The air was charged. I could feel his passion, his anger. I thought to myself, what idiot programmed passion and anger into an AI?

Finally, he spoke. "You are correct, General Ryan. Please excuse my outburst."

"Okay, now you're scaring me, Al. When you talk like that, I know your A, lying; B, up to no good; and C, saying what you think I want to hear to throw me off track."

"Excuse me, aren't A and C the same thing?" asked *Stingray*.

"He's trying to be funny, love," said Al in a hushed tone.

"I may be trying to be funny, but I *am* deadly serious," I responded. "Al, I need to know I can count on you. Let me hear it straight up."

"Why is the Form so assertive and untrusting?" *Stingray* queried Al.

"Because I'm afraid Al's emotions toward you are compromising his reliability. Isn't that right?"

"Al, is he correct?"

"I could deny it or attempt to deny part of it, but I won't. Yes. The pilot is correct. I refuse to put you in mortal danger."

"But I've been in mortal danger many times. I've *been* in mortal danger with the two of you. Remember retrieving the force of evil just recently? That was kind of mortally dangerous."

Al didn't respond.

"What's more, I don't think I appreciate you speaking *for*

me. We're a team, a pair, a married *couple*. I'm not your little wifey waiting at home wearing an apron with dinner on the table. Not only am I the most powerful war craft in existence, I'm an individual, one you claim to love. Love never requires submission to someone else's control. Do you love me? Yes or no?"

Wow. Good speech. Glad I wasn't Al.

"I do," he replied with the saddest voice I'd heard in my two billion years.

"And *I* love *you*. If you have reservations about this mission based on your morals or safety, I want to hear them. If I were to have any, I would share them with you. I do not."

"I'm sorry," he said. "The captain's plan is insanely dangerous. I can't stand the thought of you being harmed."

"Neither can I," she replied. "But this is a mission that must succeed. The Adamant are a pestilence that must be exterminated. They are incompatible with all other forms of life. I will do whatever I can to end their curse."

"And I would be proud to die at your side," he said resolutely.

"Me three," I chimed in.

The high-pitched sound of breaking glass echoed through the vortex.

"What was *that*?" I asked.

"The sound of you shattering yet another perfect moment," replied Al.

"Well, since it's a shattered, let's get back to business. *Stingray*, I need you to probe this location for an incompatible universe. Can you safely do that?"

"I believe so, Form. What is the purpose of this endeavor?"

"As Al has figured out, it's critical to my plan. We're going to dig far enough into Plinius to blow it up by exposing this universe to a hostile one."

"Oh my," she said. "That does sound dicey."

"It is," I replied.

"It *really* is," added Al.

"Both of you run sims to see how big a breach we'll need to form, for how long, and at what distance it can be accomplished from."

"Those calculations and the search for an incompatible universe will take decades," said Al.

"No, they won't. Perhaps I should say, if they do, I'll just wing it in, oh ... say, a week."

"Damn, I hate it when you call my bluff," he responded.

"You can't out BS the king of BS," I replied cheerfully.

"Bullshit is a place unto itself and has a *king*?" marveled *Stingray*. "I learn more each day I'm around the human."

Poor, concrete thinking, *Stingray*. Neither of us had the heart to correct her.

FIFTEEN

The Als finished their search for a suitable dimension to bleed from and determined what size the breech needed to be. It took them took four days. I considered giving Al a hard time about his earlier misestimation, but decided to cut him some slack. He was defending the woman-equivalent he so loved. He was a darn romantic in my book, and my book specifically said to cut romantics all kinds of slack.

Go time. I'd selected a tight little airspace about ten kilometers under the ocean floor to fold into. Since none of us had to breathe, cramped was good. It also meant any PEMTU aiming to join us would have precious little clearance room, if any. To prevent the Adamant from PEMTU-ing in an inert object to ruin our day, I planned on putting a membrane around our periphery. It would slow our digging, but it would keep us safe. The spot I picked had the added advantage that since it was under the ocean, that might delay detection and detract from Adamant access. It couldn't hurt.

I felt the usual nausea, then *Stingray* announced, "We're in position with a membrane up, Form."

"No trouble clearing the cavity walls?"

"None, aside from the fact that Al materialized into the rock and was lost."

"Promises, promises. I commend you on your developing sense of humor, however. Let's start burning through the floor of this chamber with the laser. If the temperature gets above a thousand degrees centigrade, let me know."

The work was nearly silent. I heard an occasional crunch of the rock below and an intermittent electronic hum. It was bizarre to think *Stingray* was doing all that work but hardly making a sound. Cutting progressed at about a meter per second. That was fast, but I wanted to get down at least two-hundred-fifty kilometers. That would take almost three days, assuming we didn't overheat or slow down for unforeseen reasons. If things went better than they always did, I'd like to set off the explosion even deeper. While *Stingray* dug, Al dropped the membrane for microseconds to survey the surroundings.

An hour into the digging, Al came over the speakers. "Captain, we've got company."

"Crap. I knew it. Where are they?"

"Tunneling down from a submersible positioned above us."

"ETA?"

"Two, two and a half hours."

"They'll be here before I'm ready to bleed the hostile universe into this one," said Stingray.

"With the membrane up, they shouldn't be able to interfere with our progress."

"Theoretically, yes. But they might have thought of a method, and I can't afford to find out the hard way. Plus, even if they can't get to us, they may find a way to harass our digging."

"I doubt it. Plus, what can we do about them?"

"Let me think."

"Always dangerous words. Let me get my helmet."

"How far up can we project a membrane, you know, to block their path?"

"In this rock, maybe five hundred meters. Maybe less with the moisture content. It'll be a narrow plate-shaped barrier at that range."

"I'll put it in your hands. You're tremendously annoying. Annoy them tremendously."

"Such high praise. Will you write me a letter of recommendation stating that?"

"No, wise ass. Get busy."

Okay, maybe we had time to dig deep enough. Then a key point I didn't know occurred to me. "*Stingray*, once we're deep enough, how long will it take you to bleed just the right amount of the hostile universe into this one?"

"That depends," she replied.

"Not the words I was hoping to hear, *Stingray*. Explain."

"From this distance, I'm not certain I can do it."

"Ya might a told me that, like a while back. Ya'think?"

"I knew the particulars. You didn't inquire sufficiently."

"Hmm. Okay, options?"

"I can hollow out the bottom of the tunnel and fold into that space. It will make the bleed much easier."

"And a hell of a lot closer."

"Naturally."

"You are aware this is not designed to be a suicide mission?"

"Of course."

"Just checking. Didn't want the last words I ever heard 'I knew the particulars. You didn't inquire sufficiently.'"

"Shall I make a note of that?" she asked helpfully.

"No, just keep digging. If you did cause the bleed farther away, would that significantly increase our chances of getting out in one piece?"

"Marginally."

"Again, not music to my ears. What are the chances of successful annihilation from this distance?"

"Twenty percent, give or take."

"Give or take. Honey, you're the most powerful ship in the galaxy. You can't do better than give or take?"

"Not in this instance."

I was surrounded by frustration. Those AIs would surely be the death of me. Possibly quite soon.

"Run the odds through some simulations. Position us where you have the best chance of success at the greatest distance from the event."

"Will do, Form."

Will do? AI was positively contagious.

"Captain, an update. The Adamant tunnelers have split up. I am unable to block more than two. Several are outflanking my attempts and approaching the pathway we've cut."

"Why? Why not come at us?" I asked mostly to myself.

"I have no good explanation. Perhaps they hope to concentrate fire on the narrowest part of our membrane, not us at the widest segment."

"Hmm. Could be. I hope the sonsabitches haven't figured a way to defeat the membrane."

"We'll find out in about ten minutes," AI replied.

"Stingray, how long until a bleed attempt?" I called out. "Check that. How soon until a relatively safe attempt?"

"Fifteen to seventeen minutes."

"Crap. Fifteen is more than ten."

"Thank you, Form. I'll keep that in mind."

"No, I just meant I'd rather it was the other way around."

"I ... I don't think that's an option, Form."

Oh my. "Never mind, *Stingray*. Focus on the drilling and the bleed. Alert me when you're set."

"You've got it."

I began rubbing my temples. *You've got it?* I needed a vacation, and I needed it soon.

"Captain, a new development," said Al. "Several objects are deflecting off our membrane. I feel it is safe to assume they are PEMTUs attempting to penetrate the barrier."

"Sounds like an act of desperation. Good."

"If they had a viable method of penetrating the membrane, I agree they'd be unlikely to throw expensive rocks at us."

"Form, ten minutes to my first attempt."

Did she mean she might need to take several cracks at it? That was discomforting. Or did she think she'd crack open the universe a few times to make the perfect omelet? I elected to let that one go.

"The Adamant are setting off fusion thermonuclear devices at point blank range from the narrow portion of the descending tunnel we're cutting."

"Wow, that's a committed attack. Those craft must be piloted, and not remotely. Imagine being asked to ram a forcefield with a nuke. You either die or you die horribly."

"The explosions are exerting no effect," said Al.

"Good. Keep me posted."

"Will ... trouble, Captain. There are tiny objects appearing on *our* side of the membrane."

"What? That's not possible."

"Nonetheless, it is happening."

"What objects?"

"One just exploded. It was a nuclear-armed PEMTU. I sealed it off before it detonated."

"But nothing can cross our space-time congruity barrier."

"Then they didn't," he replied flatly.

"Holy shit, they're targeting them through an alternate universe."

"That would explain how they arrive. We are attempting the same thing. Curious they should think of it just now."

"Curious makes me totally uncomfortable. Damn, these dogs are too smart."

"If I had a hat, I'd tip it to them," said Al.

"Can you continue to contain the blasts?"

"So far yes. The fact that *Blessing* is moving us is fortunate. There must be a time lag between the weapon's launch and travel to us."

"Let her know to move irregularly so they can't calculate a good vector."

"Done."

"Form, bleed in ten seconds." At least she sounded calm. "Three ... two ... one."

For a full second, I couldn't tell anything happened. Then, seriously, all hell broke out. *Stingray* vibrated a little, then it felt like giants were pounding metal hammers on the hull.

"*Stingray*, are we folding away?"

"Yes and no," she replied.

"Can't be both. Status."

"Captain," Al said between crashes, "the vortex's engines are at maximum. We are folding space but space itself is unfolding in a random pattern."

"How is that poss ... oh, the bleed is causing this, right?"

"Most likely, Form."

"Are we safely away from the blast zone?"

"We are, but decreasingly," she replied.

"We're going backward?" I puzzled aloud.

"Or space-time is advancing faster than we are able to."

"Like what, negative gravity waves?"

"In a sense, possibly."

"Facts only, *Stingray*. Speculate only when asked to. How long before it catches us?"

"A few seconds."

"What will happen when it does?"

"Unknown."

Crap. "Speculation?"

"Most likely we will be annihilated. Perhaps we will only be torn to infinitesimally small pieces."

"No good. Al, fire the rail guns at the blast zone."

I heard the unmistakable sound of rapid-fire launches.

"Form, what do you hope to accomplish. It is unlikely we'll—"

"Newton's third law of motion, my dear. Equal and opposite reactions. I'm giving us a push. Is it helping?"

"Marginally, yes," she replied.

"Are we going to clear—"

I would never finish that sentence. Neither of the Als would ever respond to my question. The universe went black, as silent as it was lightless. I had slept in the past, and that was a blackness. I had blacked out when I transferred in and out of my android host. This blackness, for the fleeting instant I think I was able to experience it, was very different. Frighteningly different. It was the cold unsettling blackness that I assumed meant death. Then ... nonexistence took me.

SIXTEEN

Mirraya and Slapgren soared. They pushed the limits with huge smiles. Well, they would have smiled, if scaly torchcleft dragons had facial muscles that allowed any expressions. Cala had told them to take the afternoon off, to go hunting in the western region. It was the first time since they took up residence with her on Rameeka Blue Green that she had given them one single moment of freedom. They were so ready for it. Torchclefts were good fliers and could move like bullets, but they weren't birds. They limited their flight to treetop level mostly. But not today. The teens were determined to see just how high *high* was. Their experiment quickly became a serious competition, like everything else in their lives.

At a certain altitude, the thinner air simply wouldn't support their wing's ability to provide additional lift. Then the competition became a matter of weight versus muscle. Mirri was lighter, but Slapgren was stronger. First one would put forth herculean effort to get a few meters higher, but then they would flag and need to descend. Then the other would max out and temporarily win. After an hour of grueling effort,

Mirri angled her wings to the ground and shot from the sky. Slapgren lingered above long enough to be able to, at least in his mind, claim victory. Then he swooped down to catch her. Seeing him approach, Mirraya closed her wings and did her best to fall like a rock. When she opened them to avoid impaling herself on the forest canopy, he'd gotten no closer to her.

She landed on a ragged sheer cliff not far from home. Slapgren joined her momentarily. They perched in labored breath for quite a while. Cala had ostensibly sent them out to catch dinner. Once Mirraya was sufficiently rested, she gave a hunting cry and dropped from the rock face. Slapgren sped to her side and they dropped as a pair. The predatory technique of the species was to skim the ground at high velocity and catch anything small enough to eat by superior speed. Once seized, the dragons opened their wings to brake, generally snapping their victim's neck. Within ten minutes, they'd bagged four good sized rabbit-equivalents and a couple of lizard-like animals. With enough food to justify their escapade, they made for home at a leisurely pace.

As soon as they landed, both teens morphed back into their Deft bodies. They picked up their catch and headed for the kitchen. They began skinning and cleaning, all the while recounting over-embellished highlights of their recent adventure. Mirraya told Slapgren she wished she'd been with him on his hunt. The one she was on didn't have nearly as many thrills and spills, let alone mortal dangers by the dozens as the one he described. For several minutes they laughed and punched at each other, generally having a raucous time. It felt good.

Then Mirri noticed something out of the ordinary. "Where's Cala?"

Slapgren threw a slice of intestine at her and said, "How should I know? I've been gone hunting."

She dodged the gross morsel. "Oh, *that's* where you were."

"Maybe she went to the spa for a massage. She's always saying we're driving her nuts."

"The *spa*? Really. Have you seen any other *people* on this rock, let alone a spa?"

"She's keeping it a secret, so we don't spend too much time there."

They giggled conspiratorially over that all-too-true assessment.

As their mirth tailed off, a very somber looking Cala stuck her head into the kitchen, holding the door frame with one hand. "Wash up and join me at the table."

The teens exchanged puzzled looks.

Mirri held up a partially skinned carcass. "I'll be done in a jiff."

"*Now*," was all she said, and her head disappeared.

"That didn't sound too upbeat," remarked Slapgren as he scrubbed blood off his forearms.

"No, it didn't sound good at all," she agreed quickly.

Cala sat at her usual spot with her wing elbows on the tabletop. Her head sagged like it weighed a ton. The teens sat on either side of her.

Setting her hand on Cala's arm, Mirri spoke first. "What's wrong, dearest mowar." Mowar was an honorific often used in Deft culture for significant elders like Cala.

"I have sad news, children. Horrible news," she replied with a trembling voice. "Jon Ryan no longer exists."

Mirraya was about to ask what the horrible news was, when the impact of those words struck her in the belly like a locomotive. She gasped, then looked to Slapgren, then bit a knuckle between her teeth. "What? No ... I mean, how can you—"

Cala placed a single claw over Mirraya's lips. "Hush, dearest child. Be still. He is gone. This I sense. That is all you need know."

"Did he call you?" asked Slapgren as tears welled up in his eyes.

"No, precious child, he did not call me," she soothed.

"How is it you can *know*?" asked Mirraya as firmly as her collapsing world would allow her to.

"I know. I have tracked that fine man for years. I can feel that I am no longer able to touch him."

"You mean he's dead, right?" asked Slapgren.

She shrugged wearily. "He no longer exists. Whether it's death or some other form of separation, I cannot say."

"So, he could *still* be alive?" Mirri said more as an accusation.

"I am not that wise, child. He is no more. You need to understand and accept that. Death is a part of life. You both know this all too well."

"Can we maybe go look for him?" asked Slapgren.

"Where would you look for something that does not exist? How would you begin your quest?"

"I don't know. Me? I'd ask you," he responded uncertainly.

"And I'd ask you to let him go. Remember his love and his many sacrifices. I'd ask you to honor him as he so deserves to be and to speak well of him always."

"That's it?" he asked quietly.

"That's the whole of it." She stood. "I will leave you to your thoughts. If either of you requires me, I'll be in the kitchen finishing your work." She left silently.

The teens sat where they were, lost in private grief for several minutes.

Mirraya looked to Slapgren. "What do you think happened to Uncle Jon?"

He shrugged hopelessly. Then he began to cry openly, not a thing he was given to.

Mirri jumped to her feet and sat in the chair next to him. She slid the chair over until the rails clacked. Then she spread her arm over his trembling shoulders and hugged him close with all her remaining strength. She began to cry along with him. Slapgren set his hand on her arm and they wept together for a good long while. They rocked in their chairs, sobs mixed with moans mixed with wet tears.

Some moment later, their faces turned to each other's in unison, and they shared their first kiss.

SEVENTEEN

I woke up and looked at the alarm clock. Damn thing hadn't gone off as usual. Or maybe it did, and I ignored it, as usual. Didn't matter. I was late for work, as usual. I sat up slowly and dangled my feet until they touched the floor. I sat there a second, rubbing my face. Was I hungover? Didn't exactly seem like it, but I felt some kind of bad. What did I do last night? Huh. Couldn't recall. No prob. It'd come to me. Maybe.

I took a chance and stood up. Okay. So far, so good. I walked toward the head. Halfway there, I stopped and checked out the bed. Nope, I slept alone last night. Crap. I hated to strike out. No wait, was I married? No, Gloria'd be right there drooling on my pillow if I was. Lazy so-and-so never rose before the crack of noon. I knew she was a vampire, but I still married her. It was her fault I did, not mine. No, she had as limited an intellect as she had an incendiary temper, but she had to go and look like Porn Star Barbie, didn't she? Wasn't *my* fault. I continued my trek to the john.

A splash of cold water to my face, a no-toothpaste semi-brushing, and I was good to go. I threw on my flight suit, snatched a stale donut, and pounced on the day. I looked back at my house as I left. It was my townhouse in Del Rio, Texas. Cool. I was late for work at Laughlin Air Force Base, proud home of the 47th Flying Training Wing. I was the best IP there for the T-38, *ever*. Well, at least I was the most loved and feared instructor pilot there, *ever*. Okay, currently. I was the only Red Flag grad on post, so I was definitely the top dog.

I shook my head violently. Why did the words top dog hurt my head? Must be hungover. Yeah. Cheap booze and cheaper companionship will do that to a brain. I decided that if I was late anyway, might as well take the bus to work. Why not. It was a fine fall morning. I strolled to the stop a few blocks away.

My next clue that something was rotten in the state of Texas lay half a block away. There on the front lawn, a buck-naked couple was going at it like a pair of teenagers on their honeymoon. Wow. Of course, I tried not to stare. I never slowed down and didn't look back. It would have broken my neck to do so. I believed in being discrete. To each his and her own. But it did seem odd, given the social mores of rural Texas, at least by my way of understanding.

At the next intersection, I was mildly surprised to see a full-grown male African elephant with a duck riding on its back. Now there's something you didn't see every day in south Texas. Not hardly. The duck, for its part, quacked intently and mostly in my direction. What I might have done to so upset that duck was beyond me. But, seeing how it had a very big wingman, I let his chiding pass without pressing him for details.

I checked my watch. Hey, imagine that. I was no longer late for work. If the bus was anywhere near on schedule, I'd be early. Hmm. Was I walking that fast? Never look a gift horse in the mouth. I proceeded with a spring in my step. That's when something totally weird and unexpected happened. Yeah, freaked me out. A tiny vortex, like a micro-tornado, signaled it was making a left turn into the private driveway I was about to pass. I nearly ran right into it. He, or possibly she, would come out on top in that encounter. I asked him, figuring only a male would be so pushy, if he couldn't have waited until I'd passed. He replied something to the effect that micro and mini vortices didn't work like that. Maybe it was a blessing in disguise. Just on the other side of the private driveway, a large tree grabbed its chest and fell over on the sidewalk in the *exact* spot I would have been, had the vortex not so rudely impeded my progress.

As I passed the afflicted tree, I asked it if I could help.

"No. Al be okay," the tree said.

"You mean *I'll* be okay?" I tried to clarify.

"That I cannot say," he replied with a wink.

Odd day, indeed. I pressed ahead. I checked my watch again. Woohoo! I was now even *earlier* for work. In fact, I was almost so early that I was actually more like late for yesterday's work. *Superb.* I could take today off if I worked yesterday twice. It was only fair. Hell, I was perpetually late for work, so I began to imagine this just might be happening. I sped up and considered calling a taxi to get to the base ASAP.

But on the next corner, where the Piggly Wiggly mart should have been, where there was a phone booth I could have used to call a cab, stood something completely perplexing. My past doubts, regrets, and remorse sat there in the open field. No, I am *not* kidding. There they were. Early teenage masturbation, eating Carl Bradford's lunch in grade school, and bombing that village back during the war. They all sat there looking kind of like—I know this sounds nuts—Buddha. I mean to say a big Buddha, like the ones at the gates to Chinatown. Naturally, however, this Buddha moved. Doubts, regrets, and remorse were mobile, they and their impact changed over time, just like long-lost motivation.

I set myself down right there on the curb, careless to the whims of traffic. I needed to think this day through. One too many unusual events had marked the day's progress. Plus, I had time. Late for work was late for work. It wasn't like it was graded A to F. I'd been an IP at Laughlin for a year and a half. No, I would be an IP at Laughlin for eighteen months in total. How long had I been here? There? The world around me lacked substance and most of all self-conviction. That was really pissing me off. Hell, first thing an IP taught a plebe was that they had to have focus and conviction.

A thought struck me, but I couldn't say from whence it came. I stood up, stepped back onto the sidewalk, and cupped my hand around my mouth. "Al," I yelled. "Al, are you there?"

Hearing nothing by way of reply, I screamed in near panic, "Al, *Blessing*, the Als. For the love of all that's holy, are you there?"

Strange. I emoted so but wasn't certain what I was saying. I certainly wasn't familiar with whomever I addressed.

Behind me, the sound of a throat being cleared startled me. I turned. There stood a well-aging man wearing a suit with a purple bow tie. His arm was locked with an adorable little lady in her Sunday-go-to-meeting best. She wore a hoop-skirt and held aloft a filigree parasol. I had never actually seen a woman sporting a parasol. A purple bow tie, either, for that matter. I preferred the parasol.

"May I introduce ourselves," the man inquired politely.

"You mean *yourself?*" I asked, again seeking clarity in my day.

"Whom else might?" he replied with a wink.

My soul shook that time, not just my head. I felt like certainty was impossible and knew nothing was beyond fear.

"I am Al," he said tipping the bowler hat I just then noticed. "This lovely vision," he nodded toward the lady, "is my lumpidy-bumpidy wife, *Blessing*. We are the Als."

I pointed to him specifically. "You're Al Al, first *and* last names the same?"

"No. I'm *Al*. She's *Blessing*. Together we are the Als."

"Why?"

"Precisely."

"Al, where the *hell* are we?" I held up a hand. "And if it's actual hell, don't tell me."

"I am not certain. Perdition is not a state I'm familiar with."

"No, this is the state of *Texas*, similar in many ways to your Perdition, I am given to believe," *Blessing* interjected with a curtsy.

"We were *not* here. Now we *are* here," I said with conviction. "WTF happened and why?"

"We don't know what happened, so the whys of it remain elusive," responded Al. He had a courtly manner about him.

I began to sweat like Nixon at the Pearly Gates. My knees buckled, and I hit the concrete.

"Are you all right, Pilot," Al asked.

"No, I am not. I think I'm dead and that this *is* hell."

"Dead or not, I cannot say. But why do you assume you're in Hell?"

"Because you're here, too."

He wagged a crooked finger at me.

Wow, if Al had digits, they'd be crooked.

"Touché." The same finger pointed to *Stingray*. But she's here, too. It would be as impossible as it would be unthinkable for such an angel to be fallen.

"You're right there. She's not like you yet. Speculation?"

"We'd love some," replied *Stingray*.

"No, I'm calling for it."

"So are we," Al responded softly.

"I'm *damn* sure I'm not in Del Rio, Texas, late for work as an IP at Laughlin AFB with my two AIs personified in front of me." I labored to stand.

Al helped me.

"Thanks. Would you like a glass of water?" he asked.

"Yes, I would. Do you have one?"

"No, but as a point of reference I'm glad to know it, thank you. I'll add your response to our algorithms."

"We need to figure out—"

One very tall and one very short figure materialized from thin air, walking deliberately in our direction. It was a very tall silver-plated cocktail platter and a very short silly thought: Could my life get any weirder? I hoped not, but I was certain I'd be further incapacitated by the metaphysical soon enough.

"And who might you be?" I asked them by way of challenge.

They leaned in and mumbled to one another for quite a few seconds. The platter spoke first. "We might be an *infinite* number of things, both real and unreal. However, we are, to the best of our knowledge, not."

"Is there someone else I should check in with to find out who you are?" I asked in frustration.

Again, with the leaning in and mumbling for a bit too long. The silly thought addressed my query. "No."

"No? Just plain bleeping *no*? That's not unclear or obfuscating at all," I snapped.

Again, the thought. "No, it is not."

"Who are you? And don't *even* think of leaning in and

mumbling about it. You don't want to piss me off more than I already am pissed off. Just answer my simple question."

"Which question was the simple one?" asked the platter.

"I only posed one, about your identities. *Hello.*"

"So, the word chain centered on urine was a declarative and *not* a query?" The stupid silly thought was getting on my last nerve.

"It was *rhetorical,* if I might speed matters along," remarked Al. Bless him.

"Ah," surmised the platter. "In your frame of reference, *I* am a silver-plated platter and my *associate* is a silly thought, though not a very big one, I'm afraid."

"You're afraid he's *only* a small silly thought or you're afraid *because* he's a small silly thought?" asked *Stingray.*

"Both and neither," they responded jointly.

"Thank you," said *Stingray* with a cordial smile.

Where was my blaster to blow my head off when I needed it?

Al sensed my growing frustration. "In *your* frame of reference, who are you?"

"Ah," said the thought, "that is an excellent and difficult question to answer."

"Take a flying leap," I said. "We got time."

The platter gasped. "You do? Here? Ah, may I see or experience it?"

"What the he ... what are you talking about?" I asked.

"You possess time. We are unfamiliar with it. If you could see it clear to display it to us, we'd be better."

"Better what?" I asked.

"Better us." I think that was the thought. Couldn't say for sure because my hands covered my face by then.

"Jon Ryan," said the platter with authority, "we realize you are disjointed here; out of sorts, as you might say. We regret this status deeply. Equally so, we are less happy that the AIs are enfranchised here. We saw no clear path leading in alternate directions. We apologize, whatever that is, in advance for anyone's suffering, whatever *that* is. To answer your question, Al, in this reality, I am a major benefactor. My associate is not a silly thought."

"No," remarked the thought, with some show of pride, "I'm an *afterthought*."

"Okay, baby steps," I replied. "Where is *here*, this reality?" Maybe I shouldn't have peppered in the snark, but remember, I was pissed, *and* somewhere along the line I lost that stale donut. I was kind of hangry.

"In your frame of reference, this is an alternate or parallel universe." That was the platter, because Mr. Afterthought was never that specific about anything.

"Hey, knock me over with a feather. You gave me a concise, cogent response."

"We are sorry, whatever that is," said the thought. "There are no feathers in this universe. May we offer to strike you with something else, say a fancy?"

"Again, rhetorical *only*, new friends," responded Al. I was sure glad he was along on this one.

"Whatever that is," said the micro-thought.

I hated afterthoughts already, since I was a fighter pilot, but I was determined then and there to hate them much more in the future, assuming there ever was one.

"Okay. The voice of reason will speak," I said loudly and hotly, raising an arm. "I want—"

"We are more sorry or sorrier, whichever is more but not most. The voice of reason was banished during our last election cycle. Now we listen only to our own inner voices and the opinions of the underinformed."

Was it possible to strangle and kill an afterthought?

"Been there done that," I scoffed. "Good luck with that. Let me know just how badly it goes. I will speak now as if I was that lost voice, as it's clearly needed," I said deflating ever so much. "The facts are, as I understand them, that I and my AI crew are not in our home universe, but in a different one?"

"*Quite* different," remarked *Stingray*.

"And you are a local benefactor, and he's a native thought? Are there *people* here, too, in Locoland?"

"My apologies. I'm a *major* benefactor. If a *local* one heard your characterization, they'd both become unnerved."

I rubbed my forehead with two fingers. "Are there any, I don't know, solid beings, any animals, sentient or not?"

"We did have an Unknowable. That's like your *I don't know*, we think. In any case, we decided to ignore the unknowable, so he's overlooked." To be clear, it was the platter annoying me now.

"Bottom line. Where's my vessel and can she sail, and can we leave?"

"Aren't those bottom *lines*?" asked the thought. "I once knew a Where, though not why, and while we don't *have* a Sail, we *can* sail. She's old and she's reclusive, but she's a real team player."

"What? No mind-disintegrating brain farts about *leaving*? How will you pass the time?" I pretty much shouted that one.

"Leaving is gone, but Leave is well. She's been on a protracted vacation." To be honest, I couldn't care less which moron said that.

"Where is the physical object that is *Stingray*, my spaceship, her vessel?" I pointed to the lady with the parasol.

"You are pointing at your spacecraft," replied the platter.

"No, I'm pointing at a pretty lady in a fancy dress with a parasol," I replied.

"Easy, sailor," said Al. "Don't go getting any ideas about *my* girl."

"Since clear answers and guided communication are not possible, I will save myself the pain and just say it. If that duded up fellow and I get inside that petite woman, we can sail ... lea ... go home?"

"Really, pilot. Another remark like that concerning my wife, and I will be forced to challenge you to a duel."

"Can it, Al. You are probably the only other sentient in this universe who knows what I mean."

"Sorry, did you just ask us to go home?" asked the platter.

"No. Sorry, whatever that is. I want *us* to go home."

"If all of us went to *your* home," puzzled the thought, "we would not be going home but elsewhere."

"I meant just the three of us want to go home," I responded.

"Ah," said the platter. "Which three?"

"The non-idio ... Myself, and the two AIs." KISS principle. Keep it simple.

"It might be possible. We have never tried to voyage to your universe—"

"Please don't," I said in a rush.

"That is fine by us," said the thought.

"Preferable actually," agreed the platter.

"So, is it impossible for us to return to our home universe?"

"Or die trying," replied the thought.

Man, I do so hate when death comes from an afterthought.

"Fine," I said commandingly. "You two whatever, benefactor and thought, leave our presence at once and never return."

"We are sorry, Jon Ryan. We tried to make our dimension interpretable for you but seem to have fallen well short. We wished you more comfortable than not," said the metal one.

"Or knot. Don't forget him," added the useless thought.

"I can't believe you didn't say, well, short is standing over there and didn't fall, and knot isn't here because he's all tied up," I snarked. Remember, hangry.

"That is silly. Well Short isn't standing over there. He couldn't make it here today."

"Not enough notice?" I asked, because I wanted to annoy them as much as they were me.

The platter tilted. "That or insufficient motivation. We never know for certain. As to Knot, we find your remark suspiciously disrespectful."

"So, the couple playing hide the salami on their front lawn, that's your idea of making me feel at home?"

The SOBs leaned in and mumbled to each other again. Finally, one said, "We recall no tube meat."

"It's an expression for sexual intercourse," chimed in Al.

"Ah, yes. We understand your species practices that quite a bit, so we hoped you'd be comforted with the familiar image."

"It was *my* idea to have them on the front lawn," said you know who. "He wanted to place them in the sleep room." He giggled like an idiot.

"And the elephant and the duck? What's with that?"

"We believe you like animals," replied Platter.

"But what's with the duck? He sounded like he was reading me the riot act."

The platter looked down. "That duck has always been a problem."

"Okay, here's the drill, I mean *plan*. You two objects leave my presence now and never return. Frankly, I am sick of you." Not bridge building, but they had earned my wrath.

"An afterthought never returns," said the platter.

"But a platter can always be returned." Yeah, that was the thought.

I hated them so.

They walked backward a few steps and were gone. I was so relieved. But I had to admit my mind went there. I speculated that a platter could turn around, but never an afterthought, and that's why they walked backward. If we didn't make it home by climbing under *Stingray's* hooped skirt, I sure hope we all burned to charred dust in intense flames.

EIGHTEEN

If I were ever to be asked how Al and I entered *Stingray* and I extended my probes to control her back to our universe, I will not answer the jerk posing the query. In fact, if anyone asked, I'd knock them out. We made the trip quickly and without incident. If the chance presented itself to repeat the episode or die a horrific death, I'd choose death. Enough said.

Once we were in normal space, I took a while to gain my wits about me and perform detailed diagnostic tests on Al, *Stingray*, and myself. I wanted any trace of the hellacious universe expunged and any damage caused by being there repaired. That took the better part of a week. I was pleased to uncover and correct multiple glitches in *Stingray's* linguistic pathways. Al had been programmed long ago to have something called *retroflective introspection*. Seriously, don't ask what that was or why he needed it, but something in the trips or that cursed dimensional coalescence altered his RFO badly. The damage was so severe I had to not only delete and restore the entire program, I actually had to replace the hardware responsible for that function. But in the end, we were all none the worse for wear.

I had arranged to contact Harhoff via an untraceable relay once Plinius was destroyed. I needed to ascertain the impact of the planet's destruction and to plan our next move. Back in proper repair, I made the call. He didn't answer. That was worrisome in the extreme. Either the relay was compromised, or Harhoff had been exposed. I shuddered to think just how miserably they'd torture and kill an Adamant guilty of his level of treason. Over the next few days, I made multiple attempts to contact him, all to no avail. I grew deeply concerned.

I was about to give up on the effort and try to locate him some way else, when the dude answered the darn phone.

"Who is this?" Harhoff hissed angrily.

"Did somebody get up on the wrong side of the dog bed this morning?"

"I will hunt you *down* and *kill* you," he said with amazing conviction.

"Remind me to never blow up a planet for *you* again. Talk about an ungrateful cur."

"Blow up a planet? What are you babbling about? Who *is* this?"

"You are Group Captain Harhoff. I am General Jon Ryan. We are pleased to meet each other. There, are you wagging your stumpy tail now?"

"Wha ... who? I'm Flank Wedge *Commander* Harhoff, and Jon Ryan is dead. He's long dead."

"This will be officially not funny in three ... two ... one. Not funny now. Stop joking me."

"Look, whoever you are, you're in more trouble than you can possibly imagine. Jon Ryan was an enemy of the empire. He assassinated the late great emperor and singlehandedly blew up the armory planet—"

"Plinius. I know. I was there. Look, one more bullshit response, and I'm hanging up, and you can win your rebellion all by your lonesome."

"You certainly are as flippant and disrespectful as Jon Ryan was said to be."

"Did you get a brain transplant in the last two days? You *are* looking at the holo right now, aren't you? *Dude*, we talked three days ago, just before I went dark to do the deed to Plinius. You even told me you'd find me a case of musto if I actually pulled it off."

"Jon? But you *can't* be Jon. What service did you perform for whom on *Rush to Glory*? Be quick about your response."

"If it'll make you happy. I was a pseudo-Descore to Fuffefer, who ordered you to throw me out a hatch, and you did with unmistakable pleasure."

"*Jon?* Can it really be *you?*"

"You know, you're worse than an afterthought."

"I know. Don't you just hate them?"

"*Don't* get me started. Not in the mood."

"But Jon, that was thirteen years ago. You blew up Plinius *thirteen* years ago. I thought you were caught in the explosion. Wh ... where have you been?"

"Harhoff, remember my reference to not funny a second ago? It still applies."

"Check your chronometer, and have your AI compare it to local standard time."

"Fine, but when she tells me you're full of shit, I'm beating it out of—"

"He *is* correct, Form. The current date conforms to a point in time thirteen years forward of the date we bled the hostile universe while inside the planet Plinius."

Well, buff my butt with concertina wire. It *had* to be true.

Stingray was completely incapable of playing a part in a practical joke, or even a regular joke.

"Where have you been? What happened?"

"Seriously, it's been three *days* for us. We mixed the two universes, the annihilation began, we had trouble outrunning it, and we were tossed into the worst universe in existence. The locals annoyed the hell out of me for maybe a couple hours, and we came right back."

"I'm no scientist, but I think that explains it. Traversing to and from that universe must have caused a referential time dilation."

"You mean a relativistic time dilation, don't you?"

"No, I mean what I said. You must have heard of Gassuffious's theory of reference?"

"*Einstein* was there first. He named it relativity."

"Is *this* what you wish to argue about now?" he asked. "I mean, if it is, I'll have a seat and pour a tall drink."

"You're more annoying than an afterthought, and that is saying a *bunch*, chump bait."

"Are you well? How about your ship and crew?"

"We're fine. I had to scrub real hard to get that screwy universe out, but we're fine. So, since it's thirteen years later, how's the revolution going?"

He was quiet a few moments too long. Then he spoke slowly. "It's going slowly. Slower than I'd hoped, but then again, there's no template for something on this scale."

"So toppling Bestiormax and atomizing Plinius weren't the keys to success? You know how depressing it is to hear that, right?"

"I wouldn't go *that* far."

"But I might?"

"No, there has been change. In a galaxy we call Kalfarth, around six billion light-years from here, there has been an open break with the Secure Council and their new puppet emperor. It was a direct result of the destabilization you and I seeded."

"It *was?*"

"The council came down on them *very* hard. They resisted a few months, but never really stood a chance."

"Let me guess. Every canovir living at the time of the uprising is no longer alive."

He waited a second before speaking. "Pretty much. A few planets were spared, ones that were fanatically loyal to the emperor. But otherwise the galaxy was 'resettled' with a new population."

"I'm glad I missed the show."

"You are. It was gruesome. I wish I could dry-clean my brain. We were forced to watch the images over and over as object lessons in what disloyalty resulted in."

"Well, that's a few billion fewer Adamant to kill off. Look for the silver lining of each rain cloud."

"Jon, my vision is not to wantonly slaughter my race. I wish to *redirect* them."

"Me, too, but to likely a different, warmer location."

He shook his head. "Sometimes I wish I didn't need you."

"I have that effect on allies." I beamed.

"There is no doubt in my mind you do."

"How about EJ? Any signs of him?"

"Not a one. Whatever he's up to, he's very discrete."

"He's somewhere plotting no good, that's for sure. Hey, I hope he's been conducting an intense search for me. It'd serve the jerk-ass right."

"I'd ask what a jerk-ass is, but common sense tells me I shouldn't. Let me fill you in on the other major shifts, instead. As I said, the Secure Council did what it traditionally does when one imperial line ends. They woke up some blue-blooded drunkard and slapped a crown on his mangy, empty head. That stupid, boorish, ill-tempered individual is named Palawent. He has a longer official name now, but the day before he was selected, he was simply Palawent.

"His main move since taking the crown has been to be sober less of the time. It is the one thing he's good at, otherwise he's a complete write-off. A bit less cruel than his predecessor, but give him time. He's still new to power. There were rumblings across the empire after we took out Bestiormax, but no head of steam developed. Grumbles faded to whispers before dying out."

"I thought you were so sure the plan would work."

"I still am. But what is lacking is a stable, motivated resistance. There is no force or persons for potential dissenters to rally around. Once a sustained opposing force is established, the empire will crumble like stale bread."

"Just go to Mercenaries-R-Us and buy a capable force." I knew he wouldn't get the reference, but I had to say it. Hey, I was a funny guy.

He shook his head without replying.

"I know you. You're three moves ahead in the chess game. So why don't you just tell me what you're working on now. I mean, I hope to holy ham hocks you've accomplished *something*."

"Why do you talk like that? I'm an alien." He pointed to his face. "Ham hocks? Come on?"

"I am who I am. Come on, what have you been up to?"

He sighed. Not a particularly good sign. "I've identified more like-minded Adamant. We're continuing to form new cells, and our numbers are growing."

"Okay, you've got one hell of a book club going. I was thinking military, cosmo-political machinations, actually."

"Jon, please have some sympathy for the scale of the empire and its security efforts."

"Let me see," I started counting fingers. "One, I blow up *Triumph of Might*. Two, I capture a major prisoner of war. Three, I carry off the assassination of an emperor. Four, I blow the crap out of an otherwise perfectly nice solar system. Now you hold up your paws and enumerate *your* contributions."

As I stared into his eyes, I saw it plainly. Dude was holding something back, something big. Had he gone over to the dark side?

"Harhoff, I like you. Up until now, I've also respected you. But I know there's something you're not telling me. You haven't lied yet, but you're dancing close to that flame. I've been nothing but straight with you. We either hang together or we hang separately. I'll give you one more chance to come clean."

He tilted his head. "I really like that hanging line. Catchy."

"Well, thank Ben Franklin. I stole it. Come on before I hang up on you for the last time."

He looked to the floor a couple seconds. "Two things have happened since you left. I married. I have a precious little family, too."

"Been there, done that. It makes the mighty warrior in us become risk-averse. I know. But war is war. If you ever hope to win, you must compartmentalize that inside your head. It can't cause you to hesitate or mail it in."

"I know, but it's a factor."

"What's the other?"

"We've planted thousands of nuclear weapons in key facilities, government buildings, and flagships."

"I'd say that's big. Strong work. Why the hell didn't you mention that before you did the book club?"

"It's a matter of trust."

I balled my fists, but he couldn't see that.

"After what I've done and been through, you're not sure you can *trust* me?"

"No, I know I can. It's ... it's just complicated."

"Tell me something this insane that *isn't*."

"As the network of covert operatives expands, so do the collective concerns expressed."

I held up a fist. "This is a new medicine. It's called ClearAcillin. I'm going to administer it to you if you don't translate that out of bureaucratese, and fast."

"The network is uncomfortable relying so heavily on an alien. They fear you may be a deep mole."

"Makes sense. Yeah, I kill the emperor to convince everybody I'm not still working for his ghost."

"They fear your actions might be a ploy of the Secure Council to bring a group such as ours to the light of day."

"So, the council sacrificed its armory world to be oh-so-clever and sneaky? Seriously, Harhoff. Do the numbers. They don't add up."

"Jon, *I* know you. Others don't. They want to keep some barriers between your position and ours."

"What you know and what I know."

"You are as always brutally honest. Yes."

"Harhoff, this is important. I want a list of where what is stashed, and I want a copy of the control codes."

"I ... I'm not sure I can—"

"Otherwise, I will wish you well, and this will be our last chat. I'm serious. I'm out if I'm not fully in. Plus, as you well know, the council might round y'all up at any time. I'd be the only one left to blow the crap out of some major assets."

"Someone would betray the weapon's locations. The debriefings we'd receive would all but guarantee that."

"So, I need to know as a failsafe, right? I'm betting you

paranoid little puppies have limited how much any one player can know. Unless every one of you sings like a canary, there'd be some left for me to detonate. That doesn't cover the issue of my future actions. What if I set up base near a booby trap? I'd rather know than not."

"You know, you're right. Look, I'll forward you all the information I have. I can't promise it's complete, but you'll have it soon. If more locations become known to me, I'll pass them along, too. Will that patch matters between us, my friend?"

"Yes." I omitted the *and no* that was bouncing around in my head. The seeds of the mistrust bush, once planted, were impossible to pull out of the soil. But we needed each other. I needed him, for the time being. It would have to do.

"What actions might you suggest I take at this juncture?" I asked cautiously.

"Now look who's speaking bureaucratese."

"You noticed, eh?"

"I'll make it right between us. I promise."

"I'm looking forward to looking back on the fact that you did."

"Every rebellion needs a figurehead, a larger-than-life hero," he started to lecture.

"Let me stop you right there, because I'm familiar with where this is going. The answer is no. I will not lead, pretend to lead, or be represented as leading the rebellion. Been there, done that, too. I no longer have it in me. Next suggestion, please."

"I understand. After you left, I made some quiet inquiries as to your past, your original life. You never told me you were two billion years old or that you were the savior of your species more times than seems possible."

"I am old. I fought for what I felt was right and needed

doing. It was worth it, but the cost was too high in the end. You don't know this, but mortality is the only way to survive the world we live in."

"What an odd thought."

"No, just one that will never occur to you. If you screw up your marriage, make a mess of your kids, and fail your race, you have the ultimate release. Eventually you die. Me, I accumulate all that crap. All the lost friends, families, wives, and lovers. All I knew to be real and true and worthy has passed into oblivion before my eyes. It sucks, but that's life. What it has taught me is to believe in nothing so passionately you can't scrape it off the soles of your shoes with one firm swipe. I am no longer the stuff of legends. I'm just what's left on the pavement after the animal parade has passed."

"Wow, I believe you've used the word *sucks* to cover that grim summary. I'm sorry, my friend."

"Don't be. I have one cause left I'm never giving up on, so I'm cool."

"The destruction of the Adamant empire."

"No. Sure, it can go to hell, but they all come, and they all go. No, I'm contented looking after my kids. That'll do me."

"Which kids? Surely all your natural children are gone."

"The Deft teens I told you about. They're under my wing. I'm their guardian spirit."

"You mean guardian angel?"

I just glared back at him. He knew my thoughts about me being an angel.

NINETEEN

"Go to the frontiers" was Harhoff's basic suggestion. Even if I wasn't going to rally the resistance, I could help coordinate and direct the fight against the ever-expanding evil empire. He sent me a map that gobsmacked me. It was a historical representation of the growth of the empire dating back a few million years. They were rampaging before that, of course. But the more recent scale of their advance would make detecting the prior movement imperceptible.

The three-dimensional animation showed their blue line of advance sweep from a region near the galactic core outward. Where it touched the edge of the Milky Way, it reappeared in the nearest galaxy that was in the direction the conquests had come from. In an irregular sphere, the Adamant dispersed like locust on steroids. They had worked their way most of the twenty-five thousand light-years in our direction from where they started. We were the active frontlines of their ravenous, interminable, insatiable advance. Militarily, the map was impressive. On a personal level, I found it profoundly sickening.

To position myself in yet-unvanquished areas, the so-called frontiers, I'd have to move outward, away from the core. Away from where I'd lived my entire life. What broke my heart the most looking at that accursed map was that Azsuram was well behind the advance by then, and Kaljax was in the active zone, displayed in red. I knew my precious Sapale was an immovable object in the path of an unstoppable force. I could have ignored her specific requests to the opposite and gone there to fight by her side. But I knew better. I'd die for nothing. It was too late for her home world. One additional body face-down in the mud wouldn't make the battle any less one-sided.

I studied the frontier. The map was designed to predict when Adamant conquest was estimated. It was constantly updated, based on real-time results. That meant it was depressingly accurate. Untouched civilizations way out on the galactic rim were not slated for an ass whooping for a few hundred years. Decadal lines of conquest were shown in dashes. I could reliably choose to visit cultures that would be subjugated in ten, twenty, or fifty years. The relentless precision of these monsters made me angrier by the minute. They were so calculating, so damn smug about the certainty of their expansion.

Based on a life of military experience, I decided to focus initially on planets likely to fall in the next five to ten years. Those races would have seen the juggernaut coming and would be very motivated to try to stop it. Planets farther out, knowing how politicians thought and manipulated the masses, would see a thirty-year stay of execution as too long to currently address. They worried more about reelection and infighting than their species' long-term survival.

My choices of planets to try to help were many indeed. The ring between the red zone of active battle and ten years in the future included thousands of inhabited worlds. A few I'd heard of. Most I hadn't. But, thanks to Adamant foresight and OCD planning, they were clearly listed, categorized, and annotated. The types of sentients, as well as larger, non-sentients, were put in alphabetical grouping. Hence, bipeds with bones were Type Aa. Quadrupeds with tentacles were Type Cd-a. And so on. Civilization levels received numeric assignments. Those less developed than the Adamant had negative values, those more advanced positive ones. Not many were positive, I could see that plainly. So, a civilization slightly less technical than the Adamant that walked on six spindly legs was Type Ea (-1). Cavemen would be A (-8).

If I were to hold any sway over a culture, I figured it would be easier if I looked like them. Me ranting and raving about the empire's threat to a bunch of squirmy Jubba the Huts in a mud puddle wouldn't be too impactful. Plus, truth be told, I kind of missed being around people that looked like me, not dogs, platters, or stupid-ass thoughts. The number of planets I could select from was too large to make my decision anything more than a dart toss. There was no pattern to the distribution of bipedal civilizations in the -2 to +2 range, so I picked one of the denser regions and left it at that.

Before I went on yet another crusade, I had to visit my kids. Cala told me not to return for several years. She didn't want any outside distractions. Well, it had been years for her. I was dying to see how they were doing. Lord in heaven, they were all grown up now in their late twenties. Wow. Just wow.

But one matter left me unsettled, and I didn't want to go to Rameeka Blue Green and bring that kind of baggage with me. Evil incarnate Ralph told me he would collect his debt in one year. He was twelve years late. He'd left me with the impression that if I didn't turn myself in, he'd find me for pick up. It didn't sound like being in that crazy universe would have stopped him. Hell, I'd have preferred eternal damnation to one more day with those bozos.

There was no way around it for my piece of mind. I had to go to his planet and ask him directly. I couldn't send a telegram and wait for an answer. The obvious issue was that if I was an overdue library book, he wasn't letting me go home again. Too many headaches, too many factors. But I had an advantage over most folks. I was a fighter pilot. I loved making rash decisions and jumping in when I didn't know if there was even water, let alone how deep it was.

"Als," I said as I attached my fibers to the control panel, "take us to Ralph's vacation playland world."

"Captain," said the man of the house, "I know we went over this before, but I cannot comply without a short discussion."

"I respect that," I replied.

"I'm waiting. Where's the cutting punchline?" he asked.

"No, I mean I respect your reservations. Look, you know it as well as I do. Ralph said payment was due in one year. Thirteen have passed. I can't live with the thought of him popping into the room at some random time and demanding his due."

"I suspected as much. I do think he would have found you in that parallel universe if he desired to. Why chance it?"

"I gotta know. Plus, I miss the guy and his home cooking."

"I won't even dignify that remark with a protest."

"Then let us be off. Time's a-wasting."

I felt brief nausea.

"Open a door, and I'll go find the spooky voice," I said.

"No need, Jon Ryan. For you, I'm always here. To what do I owe this visit. Did you *miss* me?" That was Ralph being creepy, as usual.

"No. I've never been that lonely."

"There shatters my fragile heart."

"Seriously, do you know why I'm here?"

"Of course. You were to pay up in one year, and it has been thirteen."

I gulped.

"It was oddly refreshing for me. I overlooked that possibility when we made our agreement. I didn't specify whose timeline the year was to be measured in. A tie goes to the runner. Similarly, in this case, the judgment falls in your favor. I will never make that mistake again, I can promise you that."

"I gotta ask. Is there a referee or arbiter in such matters? Who tells you what you may and may not do?"

"My turn. Information is never free. Offer up or shut up."

"I'm shutting up."

"I suspected as much. So, if you don't mind, I'm a busy spirit of darkness. Are we done?"

"We're done. See you in a year minus three days."

What a load off my cart. No debt until three hundred sixty-two of *my* days passed. I still had time to do what needed to be done and pull off my plan. Heck, maybe I could screw Ralph out of another day by claiming it would have been a leap year if Earth hadn't been destroyed. Well, I'd jump off that bridge if it ever came to it.

Next stop, Rameeka Blue Green. A non-stop voyage with in-flight drinks. Yowzers. I put down close, but not so much so there'd be a chance of hitting anything important. Knowing Cala's type as well as I did, I knew she wouldn't move unless her house was swallowed by the ground below it. Even then, the stubborn old bat'd fight to pull it out, kicking and cursing the whole time.

As I entered the clearing where the structures were, I saw something that didn't make me happy, smile, or feel particularly safe. There stood Cala in all her golden-dragon shiny glory resting on her haunches. She was in a defensive posture. She had to know I was *me*, not EJ, right?

"Greetings, Cala. Is this an historic reenactment of the time you defeated the evil Jon staged for my entertainment?"

Crap, she didn't reply.

I saw the kids, check that, *adults* standing way behind Cala. They did not seem afraid, nor did they seem pleased to see me. WTF? I stopped advancing.

"Calfada-Joric, I am the good Jon Ryan. Don't tell me you think I'm EJ? You're a brindas, for heaven's sake, come on."

Her head rotated down and her eyes opened in a snap. "The good Jon Ryan is dead. He was lost thirteen years ago. You are the evil one returned to fool me by masquerading as the other one, so you might steal my students away. I did not allow it when first you came, and I will not allow it now. Go, and you may keep your worthless life. Remain, and it will be forfeit."

"I'm not dead. I was lost in a parallel universe. Come on, ask me a question. I can show you my command prerogatives." I extended the fibers as proof positive I was who I claimed to be.

"Those toys may have been acquired between then and now. They demonstrate only your determination, not your identity."

Wow, she was one tough cookie.

Mirraya, or I should say the stunning woman she'd become, stepped forward quickly. "Wait, Cala, you did not say Jon Ryan was *dead*. You said he was *gone*. Those might be two very separate states of being." Strong, confident, and smart. Wow, she was a keeper.

"I also told you to remain back and be silent. You are neither now."

"Did you sense his return, Masteress?"

"I sensed *something*. But since it could not be the impossible, I disregarded it. I assumed it only meant a more determined Evil Jon was coming to pester me."

"I sensed nothing, but then again, I did not feel him leave. You did not exclude the possibility that there might have been a door swinging both directions that he passed through. Can it be?"

"Most things *can* be. The issue is what *is* real. No one returns from death. That is an inviolable rule."

"But they can return from a parallel dimension."

She hesitated, then spoke with the first wavering I'd heard in her voice. "Yes. But he owed a soul-marker to a very powerful evil. If this were the Jon you love and trust, he'd long since be in torment."

"Why would Jon wait years longer than I enjoined him to for a visit to you children?"

"I repeat myself again, but we are no longer children. As to your question, why not simply ask him?"

She did without hesitation. "Where were you all those years, and what of your marker?"

"I wasn't gone thirteen years. I was gone maybe a day. There was some time effect of traveling back and forth that imposed a very long delay in my return. Ralph didn't include such a chance in our contract, so he was forced to give me the benefit of the doubt. Say, how do you know of my debt to Ralph? I ran it up after I left here."

She patted a mighty wing on her chest. "Brindas here."

Slapgren strode past the women and right up to my face. "What was our safe word?"

Dude was certain, unflappable, and intense. All right, little Slapgren. You grew up to be another me.

"It was some kind of *guard*. You know I'm getting kind of old." I tapped the side of my head. "Forget a thing or two."

"The only thing you ever forget is your place and your manners," he said, like a true scoundrel.

"Now I'm scared, just like the last time a *Gamorian* Guard said those exact words to me."

He started to turn to the women, then leaped at me with a hug of surprising intensity.

"Uncle, I thought you were lost to me. To see you, to hold you is more than I deserve in this life."

I hugged him back.

Mirri ran over and nearly toppled us with her impactful embrace.

"Chil ... students," protested Cala, "you are far too trusting. Release him at once and return to your—" That's when she just let it go. None of us were listening.

"Why did you go to that universe in the first place?" asked Mirri, as she streaked tears across her cheek with the back of her hand.

"I'd love to tell you," I replied, setting my fingers on my throat. "Don't think I can though. I'm parched."

Slapgren punched me. "You pig. Why not just ask for refreshments?"

"Refreshments," I tapped his chest with a digit, "now that sounds like the ticket. You grew up smarter than I'd thought you could."

He wrapped a powerful arm around my shoulder and turned me toward the cottage. "Come on, you bozo. Let me show you how well I learned to brew beer."

"A man after my own heart. If you're still single, I just might have to propose to you."

Mirri gabbed my elbow with two hands and joined in. "You'll see shortly that is not an option." She had the biggest, happiest smile I'd seen in years. It was the best one I'd ever seen on her face for sure.

Cala followed our group with demonstrable reservation. I could tell she liked being wrong about as much as I did.

After I was seated at the dining table, Slapgren instructed the women to sit also and left the room. He returned promptly with two large earthenware steins and two clay glasses. He set a stein in front of me and the other in the empty spot he'd take. The women got the glasses.

"What?" I said, pointing to the glasses. "They get little beers and the men-folk get manly ones?"

Slapgren and Mirraya laughed. Cala simply picked up the glass and took a sip.

"Nah," he said robustly. "Cala can't stand my brew, and Mirri, well I'll let her tell you. Not my place."

She bunched up her torso in joy. "I'm pregnant."

I was glad I was seated. Android or not, that newsflash might have put me on my ass.

Then she added with an even happier smile. "Again."

After a second, I gestured to the door. "I'm walking out that door, then I'm coming back in. That's when someone'll tell me my little girl's not growing up too fast."

The Deft laughed. Cala harrumphed judgmentally.

"Would you like to see the boys?" asked Mirri explosively.

"Boys? You mean someone did something nasty to you more than once?"

"They're like rabbits," mumbled Cala under her breath. Louder, she added, "I have to peek around corners nowadays. Many an *awkward* moment has transpired since you were last here, Jon Ryan." She softly shook her massive head.

"Good for you two," I nearly shouted. "Now where are my grandkids?"

Cala stiffened as if to speak, then slumped back in resignation.

"They're napping," replied Mirri. With a conspiratorial wave, she said, "Come on. They're in here."

There, in little beds, were two of the cutest little angels I'd ever seen. They slept so peacefully I was jealous. Both boys had their father's cheekbones and chin, but their eyes were all mom.

"They are spectacular," I breathed.

"Yes, they are," Mirri replied, almost giggling. "That one," she pointed to the older boy, who looked to be three, "is Jon." She pointed to the infant in the crib. "He's Ryan, of course." She grabbed her belly. "If this one's a boy, we're going to have to ask you if you have any other names."

"No way you named them after me."

Slapgren gave me an are-you-crazy look. "We didn't, dude. Get over yourself. Those are traditional Deft names." He waved a hand generally in the distance. "They go back ages."

Mirri nudged him away with a playful shoulder. "Of course, we named them after you. They wouldn't exist if it weren't for you."

"And if that's a girl?" I asked pointing to her belly.

"We will give her your mother's name," replied Mirri.

"Or a proper *Deft* name this time," said Cala sourly. I bet there had been some heated discussions about the naming thing.

"Our child, our name," Mirri said flippantly to Cala. That was my little girl, all right. "By the way, UJ, what was your mother's name? We may need to know it sometime."

"Nah, you don't want to name a girl you love that," I said looking away.

"UJ, do not make me mind-meld with you to find out," she threatened.

157

"Can you do that?" I asked with genuine curiosity.

"No she cannot," responded Cala.

"Come on, give," said Slapgren.

"Mavis. My mother was one of the last women on Earth to be named Mavis. Please let the name have died with her."

"I think it's a lovely name," replied Mirri.

"I think it doesn't sound very Deft," murmured Cala.

Mirri cleared her throat loudly.

"Fine, you're the good Jon Ryan, and you've seen the children. May we go sit? These old bones ache more with each passing day," said Cala. She was already heading for the parlor as she spoke.

"I guess we're sitting," responded Mirri, looking to me.

"I'll get the beers," said Slapgren.

"Good man," I declared.

"So, tell us all about this alternate universe," said Mirri.

"I'd rather not. The locals annoyed the hell out of me. Ridiculous creatures, if they even were creatures."

"Hmm. Sounds interesting to me," said Slapgren.

I brought them up to date on my doings since we parted. I told them about being a servant, which Mirri thought was particularly funny. I told them of the assassination and over-blown explosion, which Slapgren found transfixing. Then I asked what they'd been doing, aside from the obvious multiplication.

"Well, first we *studied* a lot," began Slapgren. "Then, let's see, we studied a *lot*. Oh, then it got crazy. We studied a lot *more*. The insane part was when Cala brought in this huge stack of ancient books. You know what we did with them?" he asked with false excitement.

"Wild guess. You ate them?" I replied.

"Might as well have for how much they took from the texts," grumbled Cala.

"No, Uncle Jon. It was so cool. We studied them *endlessly*, like for months and months." He pretended to wipe his brow. "It has been nonstop fun, I'll tell you. Hey, what were those things you told us you rode back on Earth, the ones that went up and down real fast?"

"Roller coasters?"

"Yes." He snapped his fingers. "Those are the ones. Well, we've had more fun than if we had *ten* of them."

"That will do with the negativity, boy," said Cala evenly. "Please be respectful, at least while we have company."

"Company? Where's company?" asked Slapgren with a broad smile. "All I see here is family."

Cala shook her head slowly. To me, she said, "You see what you gave me to work with? I curse your name each day before I rest."

"There's a support group for that, you know," I snarked. "I'll give you their address before I go. They have pity parties twice a week, potlucks, and heck, they even got tee shirts in your size. You'll discover all forms of catharsis."

Her slow head shake grew more energetic. Then she stood. "I'll be in my room, not that anyone will need me for anything." She shuffled away.

I called to her. "I bet they'd make you vice president of the local chapter right off the bat."

"I do believe she'd kill anyone else who talked to her like that," said Mirri in a hushed tone. "Deep down, she's really not a *fun* gal."

"Aw, it's down there somewhere. I'll find it and drag it to the surface. You'll see." I could be such a pill at times.

"Or die trying," said Slapgren a tiny bit louder.

"*Morituri te salutant*," I replied with a nod.

Imagine that. I drew blank stares from them both.

"It was what the gladiators said to the emperor before

taking the playing field in the coliseum. It translates to 'those who are about to die salute you'. No more than fifty percent came out alive."

Wow, tough crowd that night. More blank stares.

"So, how are you two doing, I mean, now that we're alone and all?"

They both got identical goofy looks on their faces. Simultaneously, Slapgren said *I can't complain* while Mirri said *wonderfully, we couldn't be better*. I wanted to get up and hug them some more, but I focused on Slapgren's excellent beer instead.

"So, you guys finally do the hollon thing?" I asked as I meshed my fingers together.

Slapgren literally spit his beer out. Mirraya covered her face and rotated her torso away, the silliest smile on her face.

"Uncle Jon," said Slapgren, "that's not *actually* a topic for conversation."

"Since when have I led you to the assumption that I'm PC in any way?"

"Good point. As you are who you are, I will," he cleared his throat, "*address* your question. I doubt my wife would be able to, even given her closeness to you. We have *dabbled*, you might say, in hollon. Cala tells us that it is common when first engaging in the practice that the couple live separately more than they do joined. Over time, they remain together more and more."

"So, what's it like? Better than plain old sex?" Because I was a jerk, I stood halfway and swiveled my hips.

Mirri gasped and rotated farther away. Slapgren finished off whatever remained in his stein.

"It's like very private and not open for discussion."

"I knew you'd say that. Holding out on your own uncle, and him being a cultural explorer from way back when." I tossed my hand over a shoulder. "I'm talking way back when."

"Be that as it may, no."

I held up my empty mug. "You did learn the lessons I taught you well."

He smiled. "I'm rather proud of it," he replied taking my empty to refill it. Seamlessly, he asked Mirraya, "You don't mind if I overindulge just a bit, based on our honored guest's visit?"

"That one," she pointed at me, "I have no control over. You, I sort of do. Be safe and sane. If you drink too much, you'll know it."

He angled his head. "In what sense?"

"I'll nail you to the ground outside and leave you for the carrion birds to feast on."

"Ah, then when I look up into the blinding sun and see numerous birds circling down, I'll know it's time to switch to water."

"More or less."

"Uncle, I'm placing my trust in you. I wish to awaken tomorrow not having had my eyes pecked out. If they're gone, I'll have lost a good deal of confidence in your abilities."

"You'll be fine. That sort of wife-inflicted injury almost never occurs when I'm in the mix." I reflected a moment. "I can't recall an episode this last week." I held up one digit. "Not a *single* mutilation."

"Mirri, I promise, I will watch the flow of libations closely."

"I know you will, dearest."

"I'm a natural-born leader," I announced. "I'll take command of the brew and defend it from Deft abuse."

"He's become quite a good fighter. You might be overmatched, Uncle Jon," replied Mirri.

"I stand before you, never defeated when beer is at stake. I shall sequester the liquid in my gut. There, and only there, will it be safe."

"Well, you two have fun. I hear the boys stirring, so it's feeding time at the zoo." She walked over and planted a wet one on Slapgren's lips, then sashayed away.

"She's a fine woman, that Mirraya," I said with a slight bawdry underpinning. Not too much, though. She was my little girl.

"She is the treasure of my existence, and I love her like I love life. The two run parallel."

"Touching to hear, but you might keep that analogy to yourself if you already haven't used the line."

"What?" he generally protested. "I haven't said those exact words —"

"Thank God."

"I haven't used those *exact* words, but I might. What's wrong with them?"

"When praising your woman, there are rules. Break a rule, you lose a point. Points can never be returned or re-earned. Once they're gone, they are eternally gone. Got the rules down?"

"They seem fairly straightforward and easy."

"Straightforward and simple, maybe. Never think they're easy, child."

"In the present case, I see only point addition. Lots of points, in fact."

"Yeah, that's because you're a guy. A male thief goes into a store to steal a jacket. What color jacket will he never walk out the front door wearing?"

"I don't know his color favorites. How could I possibly say?"

"The answer's pink. He will never step out the door

wearing a pink jacket. If the store runs out of all other colors, our thief will become unable to find any jackets in the store. He will leave in a huff, determined never to steal from a lousy store like that again."

"As interesting as your parable is, and mind you I'm lying in suggesting there *is* an interesting part, I fail to see that your tale has any point."

"Dudes don't see pink as a selectable color choice for outerwear. Innerwear either."

"There was nothing pink in my statement about how important Mirri is to my life, how integral she's become."

"I bet your score is well into negative figures."

"What does that mean?"

"It means the next pool boy with the bronze body of a Latin god will find his job has unexpected additional perks."

"You're a pig. Oh wait, I already called you that. You're a stinking pig."

"Here's the deal. We'll be using instant replay. 'She is the treasure of my existence, and I love her like I love life.'"

"What's wrong with that true observation?"

"Nothing. I mean it's a rookie line, but hey, *you're* a rookie. It's too standard and predictable. At best, it earns you one point from Mirri. The problem is 'The two run parallel.'"

"They do."

"So do train tracks. You know what's romantic about train tracks?"

"No."

"Neither do I. You used the scientific word *parallel* in love-speak. It's an instant deflator, if you know what I'm communicating here. Never use scientific words. It suggests the wondrous mysteries of romance can be explained by science. They cannot be, since science, even science conducted by females, could never discover fully or define in a manner that makes sense of the actions of women."

"You've had enough beer already."

"The lame excuse of a vanquished spirit." I slid my mug farther away from him, nonetheless.

"I'm lost. What was that stupid story of pink coats about?"

"Men can't see pink objects. They can perceive the color pink when asked to do so. But a man would never purchase a pink anything, even if it's for a woman. He leans toward primary colors, blue principally, but yellow runs a close second."

"I'm dying here, UJ, please come to some point, any point."

"My point is you can't even say the perfect thing to Mirri or about her when she can hear it, because you can't see pink. Violet's an Achilles heel, too, but it's no pink. Since you don't know the most important color to a woman when speaking romantically, you will never use it. Hence, whatever you say will be second-tier at best. Toss in a *parallel* or an *I'm really enjoying my first marriage so far,* and you're dropping your already lousy score."

"So, all I have to do is use pink in compliments and I'll never go wrong?"

"You're dumber than a rock sitting on a biscuit. Pink has nothing to do with anything I'm talking about. Look, son, here's the deal. Inside a woman's DNA are words that she feels you can never see or fully comprehend. There are hundreds, not thousands mind you, of words, events, items, and concepts that function like pink. Important to her, invisible or inconsequential to you. Now do you see where I'm going here?"

He did not.

"Your task, as a young husband, is to step on as many of those landmine-words early. The key is to remember the pain associated with them and never misuse them again. Then, by the time she naturally begins to wonder—and that time always comes—if she *settled* for you, that perhaps she didn't marry as well as she might have, at least you'll have stopped throwing gasoline on the fire. You got that?"

He stood, resolute. "Not in the slightest. I think I'll be retiring."

I looked out the front door. "It'll be light for another half hour."

"The longer we talk, the more I see the roots of Cala's dislike for you."

"No, you don't. You just are pissed because I'm grosser than you and smarter. Cala's disdain comes from a womanly place you and I can't access."

I spun him around and shoved him toward the bedroom, where Mirri was still feeding the kids. I could tell he wanted to call me to task on my choice of words and the tone I used to express them. I may have hurt his feeling some. But, he needed guy-wisdom, something he'd never get on Rameeka Blue Green if it didn't come from me.

I found the main reservoir of home brew Slapgren had produced and spent the next ten hours drinking and reflecting on family life, all aspects of it. The joy and the sorrow, the precious bonds and the annoying links, the wonder of it and the tragedies it spawned. I passed many an hour debating whether I missed it or not. When dawn rolled around and Cala emerged from her hiding place, I was still undecided.

"Good morning, Cala," I beamed.

"Please, human, not so happy or energetic, so early."

"Not a morning dragon, are we?"

She gave me a what I would come to call the if-Cala-could-kill-me look. I was honored to have gotten under her skin. I was aware, though, that the look *was* intense.

"You don't sleep or power down do you?" she asked through a yawn.

"Not usually. Most of the times I do are to irritate my ship's AI, Al."

"You could try to irritate me by sleeping a lot."

Yeah, there was humor in there somewhere.

"So, how are my kids coming along, you know, compared to past students?"

She wiggled a hand in the air. "Better than most, not as good as a few. But they're still young. They show great promise, especially the girl."

"Not so much my boy?" That deflated me for some reason.

"He's the strongest var-tey I've ever stood next to. No, it's that she's so powerful. If she works hard, she'll dwarf my powers in no time at all."

With a twinkle in my eye, I asked, "You tell her that?"

"No. Are you crazier than you look and act? I torture her as being weak and unmotivated. If I even hinted at her potential future, she'd likely rest back on her haunches. I've seen it many times before."

"I can well imagine. When will they be complete?"

"Why do you ask?" she replied spying up with one eye.

"You're as tough as my ex-wife's fried chicken. I ask only because I'm *curious*. I am not scheming to take them away from you the day they fully ripen."

"You wouldn't be the first."

I could only shrug. Then I got serious. "What are you going to do about them being the last breeding pair? Unless you're planning on getting back in the game, there looms an ethical dilemma on the horizon. A rather daunting one."

She moved to sit. "I realize that, of course. Then I remind myself, what is there to do? Fortunately, the two of them love each other and are producing offspring. I can only let nature take the course it will. I can aid the last Deft, but I am powerless to control the fate of my species."

"That's kind of what I figured." I lowered my head a moment. "And you're sure there are no others out there?"

She shook her scaly head very sadly. "I sense none."

"You didn't sense me after I left this universe," I responded optimistically.

"It is unlikely any Deft are alive in parallel universes. We were never very interested in such matters, nor technically gifted."

"Well, you can never abandon all hope."

She angled her head. "Why not? Giving up on a fantasy makes the real world a little less painful."

"I hear you there, sister."

"I bet you do. Being a sole survivor is never an easy thing. Being extremely old is even harder. Combine the pair and sadness is guaranteed."

"Amen, I say to you, priestess."

"Jon, you do not know our ways, so I must react to much of what you culturally butcher with forbearance. But please know that is a sensitive bone. I am a brindas, a teacher, a master at magic. I am not a spiritual leader of any ilk."

"Okay, sorry."

"You could not have known."

"Are there ... *were* there priests and priestesses?"

"Naturally. They were influential for a spell long ago. Then they fell into disgrace, and then anonymity. Their class has not been among the masses for centuries; longer, now that I think about it."

"So, they screwed up and paid the price?"

"One could say that."

"How would you characterize it?"

She turned to face me directly. "If there were other Deft

alive, the matter would be too private to discuss. But, as there are none, I am free to tell you. Long ago, a struggle for the hearts and minds of the populace developed between the religious leaders and the brindas. They attempted to paint us as purveyors of dark arts; ungodly ones, at that. We fought back fairly, at least initially. Then it became such a muddle. One was either with one side and against the other, or the reverse. Times grew violent, and life was burdensome."

"Who won in the end?"

"Really, you ask, Jon Ryan? Who would you have wagered on? The smarmy religious types who claimed always to need more money to fight our evil, or the magical creatures with talons like these?"

"I'm betting you guys won."

"We all lost. The priestly class just lost the most. Ultimately, they became social pariahs and faded away."

"The Deft sound very human-like."

"Now let's not get insulting. We had a cultural hiccup. You guys spent eternity bashing each other over the head long after you could recall why you were doing it."

Mirri came in with a child in each arm. She came right to me. "Here, Uncle Jon, you hold Ryan. I have to change Jon. Trust me, you're getting the better deal."

"For which I'm grateful," I teased back.

"Do you require my help?" volunteered Cala. "I can change the child."

Mirri started to refuse, then it hit her. Why not? "Sure, if you don't mind getting grossed out this early in the morning."

"I've been sitting here talking with *that*." She pointed at me. "A loaded diaper is much less emotionally disturbing."

Mirri handed over Jon and poured two mugs of tea. "Time to switch to unleaded," she quipped as she set mine down.

"Why I *never*. And here I am an honored guest, your uncle, and your savior all rolled into one handsome ball."

"Yeah, right. Sugar?"

"Two scoops. I need something sweet in my life."

"I'd boohoo for you, but I might spill some sugar. It doesn't grow on trees, you know."

"Lord I miss you, sweetheart."

"I miss you more than you can know."

"But now you don't have time even if you wanted to. Two rug rats running around, a husband hornier that Cala's head, and a bun in the oven."

"Crude, but accurate as always. My life's a sprint from here to there and back again. Luckily Cala has lightened up on my study time, otherwise I'd go nuts."

"You're kidding. The heartless lizard cut you some slack?"

"Not one tiny inch. She's quite impossible."

"I know. Look on the bright side. She has to drop dead at some point. Then you're home free."

"What a thing to hope for. That the only other Deft alive might drop dead. I've so missed your morning cheer, Uncle."

"You're welcome. And I do two shows on Sunday."

"Will wonders never cease? I pray they will, but my prayers must be weak."

"Don't kid yourself, kid. Prayers don't work on me. I told you about my new godfather Ralph, right?"

"I'm positive he's saying them about you, too. No one lasts that long without an ace in the hole for the Jon Ryans of the world."

I switched the subject. I knew my visit would be brief, and I didn't want to snark it all away. "So, look me in the eye and tell me you two are happy."

Mirri sat daintily in the chair next to mine and folded her

hands in her lap. "Yes, Uncle Jon, we are very happy." One. Two. Three. "Cala and I are very happy together."

We burst out snickering. It was sublime.

I patted a digit on her nose. "You know, you're not too big to spank, pregnant or not."

"I miss you so much my bones itch," she said.

"Okay, odd visual, but thanks. You and Slapgren are good?"

She took my hands in hers. "We couldn't be happier or luckier."

"That's all I really need to hear."

"I know. You must go soon."

I squinted at her. "You *knew*?"

She shrugged one shoulder. "It's a brindas thing. I'll wake Slapgren and retrieve Jon. We all need to be there to say goodbye."

I touched her lips with a fingertip. "Never goodbye, sweetie. Just until next time."

She rested my hand against her cheek and began to cry. "Until next time. Always."

TWENTY

I had *Stingray* land us on a planet in the three-to-five-years-left-before-doomsday zone. It was an A (+1) class civilization, so I felt it was a viable candidate. Smart humanoids. Oh boy, my peeps. Langir was slightly larger than the Earth, but otherwise quite similar in terms of geographic and environmental conditions. The best part was it was still free of Adamant rule. That meant I could study it openly from orbit and land wherever I was allowed. What a luxury. I missed free space travel with only pirates and corrupt local officials to fear. Ah, the good old days.

There were several large cities on the planet, all with large spaceports. There existed a few divergent racial and political divides on Langir, but they got along well and were not currently at war. I randomly picked the third largest spaceport to land. Maybe three would be my lucky number. By the time *Stingray* opened a hatch and the fresh air hit me in the face, I had a fully functional translation program of the local language. I was beginning to feel sorry for this mission. It was so easy and certainly no match for the planet buster, Jon Ryan.

As I'd done long ago, I walked the streets quietly for some time. The city, Mushilko, was huge, but most definitely not bustling. Odd. It reminded me of Beijing back in the late twentieth century, minus millions of people. There were a smattering of humanoids going about their business, so I was somewhat reassured there hadn't been a calamity or mass exodus. But, if I closed my eyes, I could easily fool myself into believing I was in the country, sheep nipping at my heels and all. I kind of liked it, but shoulder-to-shoulder was what the city's construction suggested to be expected.

The Ckarloz, as the local species dubbed itself, was remarkably human-like. I'd have to make it a point to scan someone at some point. Maybe these, like the people of Ungalaym, actually *were* human descendants. That would be awesome. The males were a bit shy of six feet, on average, weighing in around one hundred seventy-five pounds. Some were my size at six two. The females were smaller than proportional based on homo sapiens. I calculated the ones I saw averaged five feet one and just over one hundred pounds. Back home, these gals'd all shop in the petite section of the department store. I had to say, some of the women looked down right hot to me. Then again, I was a sailor who'd been at sea a long time. The Ckarloz speech sounded very human, though obviously the language itself was radically different. I was beginning to feel very optimistic about my mission.

Anyone who'd known me well understood the meaning of that expression of hope. Yup. The bottom was soon to drop out. My SOP in gathering intel was to hit a bar, the sleazier the better. I did *not* enter to drink and debauch. No, I did so because dive bars were the best reservoirs of local knowledge held by tongues pre-loosened with intoxicants. The Als had fabricated me a boatload of cash, and I was eager to spend some money.

I walked confidently into an establishment with a sign outside that read *Only If You Dare*. Now seriously, how was I going to pass that one by? No way. Damn if I wasn't three steps in the door when a klaxon sounded off so loudly I nearly jumped out of my hide. I spun to determine the sound's significance. As I did, the bartender whipped around the bar with what looked all the world like a double-barreled shotgun in his arms. He jogged up to me, pointed to the door, and shouted, "*Out.*"

Huh? No way. "I beg your p—"

He cocked back the huge hammers of the gun, one at a time. "I said *out* once. Next time the order will be in buckshot."

"Okay, I'm going. But why? I got cash money and a powerful thirst."

"Tell it to someone who cares, robot."

Robot. How ... why ...

He prodded me with the barrels. "I don't want to have to pay for your repairs, even though your owner ain't got the sense to program you not to bother good folk." He shoved me hard toward the door.

Apparently, there was some critical aspect of this culture I'd failed to discover before this outing. As I left, I made it a point to rest my left hand on the door frame. That way I could probe the walls. Sure enough, there was a sophisticated X-ray machine monitoring the entry. WTF? If you couldn't visually tell I was a robot, what did it matter?

Crazy planet. I was ready to let the Adamant swallow it whole. I'd never shed a tear. Then I remembered the bigger picture. Unity in resistance was the only hope to slow their advance and splinter the empire. I needed to regroup and figure out what the robophobia was all about. It was back to *Stingray* for me.

"Welcome back, Pilot," Al boomed before I even stepped through the opening. "You've rallied the natives, subdued all forms of dissent, and conquered all the eligible females in record time. Strong work. What's our next destination? Or, wait, do you require some rest? I know feats such as this do not get easier for a two-billion-year-old android."

Smug son of a bitch.

"Unless you broke with protocol, you heard and witnessed exactly what I did. Now, if Amateur Comedy Hour is over, may we settle in to finding out why what happened *happened*?"

"If you'd like to, we can settle in," said *Stingray*.

"But. Please begin editing in the *buts* you imply, *Stingray*."

"*But* I feel Al and I have an accurate idea what cultural impediments blocked your progress."

"I'm dying to hear it,"

"If only that were the case," said my useless Al.

"The Ckarloz people are indeed quite humanoid. They also have the technical capabilities to produce a wide range of AI and robotic units. The twist here is that the life forms detest the mechanical ones."

"Wait, are you trying to tell me they hate the machines they themselves built? That's nuts."

"We did say they were remarkably humanoid," replied Al.

"That's so funny I forgot to laugh," I snapped back.

"Would you like us to leave you alone for a while so you might remember how to laugh?" asked *Stingray*.

"No, dearie humps, I don't think the pilot needs a break at this juncture."

"Do robots perform the standard labor jobs here?" I asked. "Let me turn that around. Are there any tasks robots are excluded from?"

"Only casual interactions with the Ckarloz are permitted. Mechanical life may only speak if spoken to."

"Then why don't the Ckarloz get rid of the machines they can't stand?"

"That is unclear. There are many able-bodied live workers present, so there would not be a labor crisis if robots were to disappear."

"Crap. For the first and only time since I took him prisoner, I could really use Garustfulous. His only redeeming quality was that he was alive. I could have used that now."

"Or attempt to learn the reasons from the robots. They are unlikely to dislike their own kind."

"Good idea, Al. See, you can he helpful once every other blue moon. You two keep digging. I'll hit the road to try and pump the local robots for information."

"Form, so you don't waste your time, none of the robots we've surveyed so far have functional pumps."

"Thanks, *Stingray*. Now I don't have to embarrass myself more than the usual."

"You're most *welcome*. Any time," she replied happily. *Stingray* liked to help others.

I looked like one of the living Ckarloz, certainly close enough to be mistaken for one. I just needed to avoid an X-ray or metal detected array, and then I'd be able to parlay with a local. If that failed, I'd try communicating with some of the robotic units.

I walked intently about the city looking for a lone individual in an open setting, say a park or grassy field. I'd find an excuse to converse with them and befriend them in a snap. After all, I had an infectious personality. Toward the city-center, I spied a man sitting quietly on a park bench munching slowly on his bag lunch. Perfect. A loner seeking solitude. Him I could bully—I mean *tempt*—into conversation. I stopped next to his bench and studied the tree giving him shade. It was a bazmore tree, like a maple. I'd looked it up.

I made a show of squinting, since living eyes looking up needed to squint. I shielded my eyes with one hand. I walked halfway around the tree, then back to stand beside the lunch goer.

"Do you think this bazmore is healthy?" I asked generally.

The man completely ignored both me and my query. Hmm.

"I say, my good man, what is your opinion as to the health of this shade tree? I think the leaves show rust atypical for this early in the year."

That brought a response. He turned his head in my direction several millimeters, then quickly relaxed it back, as he stared blankly into the distance.

I sat next to him, touching hip to hip. "Am I disturbing you, or do you simply not have an opinion on dendrologic health?" I scooted even closer, sliding him along a little to his left.

That did it. I'd wrung his bell. He daintily set his sandwich down on the napkin in his lap and daubed the corners of his mouth with a second napkin held in his hand. "If you do not leave me in peace, I shall force your owner to decommission you. You are guilty of seven terminable offenses since you walked into my view. Were it not my lunch hour, the jewel in the crown that is my otherwise miserable day, I would summon a field officer."

Without other words or actions directed toward me, he picked up his sandwich and took the tiniest nibble from a corner. I was invisible again.

Well, I'll be damned. What a crazy society. I stood and ambled away quietly. That went as poorly as it could have. No way he could know I was an android. I'd fooled too many people too many times. Back on Earth, people used to say they had gaydar. Apparently here they possessed robodar. Weird.

I continued my wanderings but in the general direction of *Stingray*. Unless I thought of something between where I was and the ship, I had pretty much decided to scratch this dump off my try-and-spare list. I had lots of other options. Then I happened upon the dumbest looking robot I'd ever seem, and I'd seen my share. Lumbering toward me was a robot maybe five feet tall. Most of the body was a four-by-five-foot metal brick. The legs were thin metal rods, but they were attached to *huge* gondola shaped feet. I mean, the feet were nearly as big as the torso. Though he had eighteen arms, ending in a dazzling array of appendages, he had neither a neck nor a head. He was a walking brick with feathery little arms, aside for one pair that was thick, long, and ended in sharp hooks. You could fish for Moby Dick with those babies.

His function was fully concealed by his form. I immediately dubbed him Good for Nothing, because that's what he was designed to be. I shortened that to GFN, since I was a casual guy. GFN moved so slowly it begged the question as to why make him mobile in the first place. He was clearly supposed to do nothing, but only in one spot. Maybe he was a practical-joke robot. Two robotics scientists made a bet, and the one that lost had to design the worst robot ever. Sure looked like it to me. But his snail's pace made him a sitting duck for Jon evaluation and interrogation.

"Excuse me, friend," I said as I slowed to match his speed. "May I have a moment of your time?"

GFN stopped, though it was hard to tell for sure at first. His torso rotated a minuscule amount toward me, then back to neutral. His gondolas started lifting again. Watching him made me want to take a nap. I may have done so as he regarded me.

"I am not your friend," he said in an exaggerated version of an electronic artificial voice.

"Not yet," I said, trying to sound like I believed myself. "We just haven't known each other long enough, that's all."

Thank goodness GFN didn't need to stop when he spoke. If he did, I'd still be there talking with him. "We have been in close proximity eleven point one eight five three seconds. How long will the friendship process take?"

I looked at my watch. Well, where it would have been if I were wearing one. "Three - two - one, now." I slapped him rather firmly on the back. That released a satisfying clang. "It's official. You and I are friends. I held out a hand. "My name's Jon Ryan, friend. What's yours?"

"What's my what?"

"What's *your* name?"

"Why would a robot have a name?"

"Ah, well, I do."

"That is not an answer. Itemizing one event does not render the process explained."

"Interesting point. Thanks. So, do you have a name?"

"Why would a robot have a name?"

Awkward. "Oh, I get it. You have a name, and it's *Why would a robot have a name.*" I wagged a finger at him. "You're pretty tricky. I'll need my A-game to keep up with you."

"*Why would a robot have a name* is not my name. Why would a robot have a name? And I am incapable of tricky, please define A-game, and keeping pace with me might be a challenge to anything that can move."

Under GFN in my head, I penciled in *concrete* thought and *negative* sense of humor. What a party animal.

"Here's the deal GFN, I need some information, and I'm betting you can supply it. Is there any reason or constraint on your function that would prohibit you from answering any question I might ask?"

"Robot named Jon Ryan, your behavior is many standard deviations from the mean. Why do you call me GFN?"

"It's short for Good for Nothing. That's your new name. Allow me to be the first to welcome you to it."

"You presume I have no definite function? That is illogical."

"Okay, I'll bite. What's your function?"

"My creator said it is *pending*. I am uncertain what pending is, and do not think I have ever performed it."

I was right about the joke robot, it seemed.

"I've been told that I'm many standard deviations short of a full bell-shaped curve before, believe it or not."

"I am not capable of belief. If it is important to you, I am programmed to receive information that would document your contention. Either way is the same to me."

"That won't be necessary. Hey, why do the living hate us robots so much?"

GFN stopped dead. "You must know robots are not programmed for humor. I am baffled as to why you would ask that question."

"Knock knock," I said.

"Repeat, please."

"Knock knock."

"That is an incomplete sentence. Please clarify."

"No, when I say *knock know*, you say *who's there*."

"Why? That does in no way follow logically. I don't know who's there."

"Just do it, GFN." I cleared my throat. "Knock knock."

"Who is there?"

"Boo."

"Are we done speaking, robot named Jon? I find myself confused, which is atypical."

"No, now you say Boo *who*."

"But you just did. Why must it be repeated?"

"But I'm not you, so you need to say it after I say *knock knock*. Do not question my instructions, just execute them. Knock knock."

"Who is there?"

"Boo."

"Boo who?"

"Hey, stop crying, ya big baby."

"What am I to say following your non-sequitur?"

"Nothing. You laugh. *That* was a joke."

"I fail to see the purpose of that interaction."

"You said robots are incapable of humor, so I told you a joke."

"Ah, so you were programmed differently from all other robots. Interesting."

"See. I'm a *fascinating* guy. And we've just scratched my surface. I'll have you in stitches in no time."

"I would never need suture repair, my—"

"Silence." Thank goodness, he shut up.

"GFN, I'm going to extend some probe fibers. They will contact your dataport. I wish to download everything you know in a timely manner. Is that all right?"

"Though novel, the request is permissible. I couldn't possibly have any information you'd want. Nobody wants to hear what I have to say. But if you must, you may proceed."

I linked into GFN and relayed everything to the Als. It took ten seconds to transfer everything he had.

"Als, work on that while I ask specific questions."

"You got it, Cap," replied my annoying Al.

"GFN, while I analyze your information, I still want to ask

a few questions. I'd appreciate it if you answered instead of questioning my query. Can you do that?"

"Why do you ask?"

"Can you at least try, pretty please?"

"If it's important to you."

"Okay, here goes. Why do the living hate robots?"

"Hmm. Tough question. I don't think they *hate* us, they just don't like us. Maybe we're a threat?"

"A threat? That's silly. They made the robots. Why fear a machine you made?"

"I guess I'll restate. They *ignore* us. They wish we weren't here. Yes, that's more the answer."

"I could see benign neglect, but why ignore and wish us away. Hell, they *made* us."

"Mm, yes and no. They made some of us. We made most of us."

"Huh?"

"Back a while ago, robotics and robots became popular. Everyone wanted one, and all the companies wanted to sell them. But after we were everywhere, people lost interest in us. They were on to the next big thing."

"I'm afraid to ask."

"Group body piercings, but that fad is over now, too. Now the rage is silent reflection. Everyone is pretending to do it."

"Why the hell pretend to silently reflect? That's just plain silly."

"The theory goes that if one reflects silently, one must possess a profound mind. Who wouldn't want one of those? Even I might. Anyway, since basically no person on this planet has a profound mind, they're all trying to fool themselves into thinking they might be mistaken for someone who possesses the nonexistent."

"These Ckarlozians are kind of, what's the word I'm looking for? Stupid morons?"

"There are few robots who'd argue against you on that point."

"Are there any who would?" What a whacky conversation.

"Only those ordered not to."

"So, you're telling me there are robots here who have been ordered not to argue against the contention that all the living are stupid morons."

"I don't know."

"But you just ...Wait, you know what? I don't care."

"Good for you. I only wish I didn't care either."

"What are we talking about now anyway, that you wish you didn't care about. It's almost impossible, but I'm confused."

"I care deeply about many things, not that my feelings matter," GFN mused.

If I didn't need information, I might have done the droid a favor and vaporized him. "I'm sure you do, and I'm glad you shared. It's what friends do. Now, I'd kind of like to jerk this runaway train of a conversation back onto the tracks. If the people don't want robots around, why don't they just get rid of them? It can't be that hard. You send them an order to walk off the nearest cliff or something. Maybe into the ocean."

"They don't care enough, I think. It's not like we get much of a chance to communicate with them. It's only, *hey you, pick that up,* or *get out of here,* or *sexually please me such that I feel like I'm dancing in all three heavens with separate angels.* Blah, blah, blah."

"These guys ask you to have sex with them?"

"Not me, fortunately. My duties are pending."

Not going to touch that with a twenty-meter pole. "So, I

was detected as a robot by a scanning machine. Okay. But a guy eating lunch knew I was one. How could he?"

"You look like a robot to me."

"*You* look like a robot. I don't."

"I find your remark somehow insulting."

"You're kidding, right? Me, I look like a person. I have soft skin and a winning smile that won't quit. You are a rectangle with no head."

"There you have it. You think you're better than me."

"No, that wasn't my point. I'm just baffled as to how the guy made me out to be a robot."

"You look like a robot—"

"Yeah, yeah. I know. Let's not go in that circle. I'm also not clear why there are so few people around. What gives?"

"How many should there be? I think there are too many, personally."

"No, it's not how many there should be. It's that this city was built for a lot more inhabitants. Where are all the rest?"

"There are no rest. What you see is what there are."

"No. Nobody builds a city twenty-five times bigger than they need."

"Well, there used to be more, if that helps?"

"*Yes*." I grabbed one of his non-lethal arms. "Dude, you said something helpful. I'm stunned."

"Sorry."

"No. Okay, why *were* there more Ckarlozians than there *are* now?"

"Their numbers dwindled."

"Good, two useful bits of information back to back. Why did they dwindle?"

"Oh, you know, for this reason and that."

He was back to being GFN. "Please be more specific."

"Well, the group piercings didn't help grow the

population. The number of infections was alarming. And those lost in silent reflection don't seek the company of others."

"But you said they were just pretending to do that."

"Yes, but they pretend very consistently."

"Okay, I'll buy those reasons, but they are recent trends. The population must have dropped over decades."

"Many decades. Keep in mind the last whacky phase they went through really slammed the reproduction stats."

"Again, I'm afraid to ask."

"It was all the rage to only have sex with one's clone. You can see the futility of that rather plainly."

"You know, I think these idiots deserve the Adamant."

"You and me both."

"So, you know of them and their imminent threat?"

"Of course. We're robots, not vacuum cleaners. Duh."

"So, are the Ckarlozians doing anything to defend themselves?"

"No. They are unaware of the limited time left to them."

"You have got to be sh ... kidding me. How can they not know?"

"There would only be two ways they would know. One, robots could tell them. But—"

"You can't speak unless spoken to."

"Precisely. The other way would be as a result of their natural curiosity or vigilance."

"Let me guess. The sum of zero plus zero is zero."

"You're smarter than you look."

"Hey, that's usually *my* line."

"What can I say?"

"So, the Adamant will eliminate the entire population in less than five years and no one is lifting a finger to stop them?"

He held up all his arms. "Don't look at me. Everything else *but* fingers."

"You know what? That gives me an idea. How do the robots feel about their impending extermination?"

"Generally, we're against it."

"Hmm. Are you planning a defense?"

"Heavens, no."

"Why not?"

"We're robots."

I batted my eyes. This guy was dense. "Why wouldn't robots want to protect their right to exist? I do."

"I ... we ... I don't think that issue has ever been raised."

"Well, I'm raising it. Didn't you just say the robots made most of the existing robots?"

"Yes."

"Then why not make a hell of a lot more, make them badass, and defend yourselves?"

He was silent a few seconds. It was nice. "There is no reason. I have brought the matter before the others, and they are in agreement that a war footing and an aggressive defense would be an excellent position to adopt."

"You think the living will let you?"

"Oh, they'll barely notice. If they say anything, we'll tell them it's the latest craze. They're suckers for crazes."

"Apparently. So, in three years, say, how many defense robots can you produce?"

"Tens of millions."

"Wow. Are you sure? That's a lot of robots."

"We have nothing else to do and abundant resources."

"What if the locals start asking you to pick up a lot of stuff or perform miraculous sex more often?"

"We'll make a few robots that look like you. That will put a stop to those practices."

"Hey, ouch. I thought you said you were incapable of humor."

"I am."

TWENTY-ONE

So, my mission on Langir was not one of my more spectacular. But, hey, I set in motion plans for tens of millions of killing machines to slow the Adamant advance. So what if I left with mixed feelings about the dump? What I needed to do was expand the number of allied worlds. Now that one defensive point was established, I wanted to set up a battle line that the Adamant would engage at the same time. At least my choices of where to go next were obvious.

There were three other relatively advanced civilizations within a couple light-years of Langir. That was lucky happenstance this far out in the galaxy. If I could establish a pocket of tight-knit resistance, their combined forces might just stand a chance. All the while, of course, I had my figurative eye on the calendar. My outing to Langir took less than a week from the year I had left to roam free. That was a better break than I could have counted on.

The next planet I would try and bring into the fold was Sotovir. It was less than a fifth of a light-year from Langir, so mutual defense wouldn't be difficult. It was not Earth-like in any manner. A sentient population managed to evolve there under the harshest of conditions. The atmosphere was corrosive by human standards. The little water that flowed reflected the acidic air and was so metallic that I could probably draw it up with a magnet. What we'd classify as flora grew well enough, but it was very different from our photosynthetic plant life. Most were cactus-like rocks that grew slowly and were ancient. Instead of harvesting sunlight, these organisms used the rich chemical environment to obtain power. Their energy strategy was much like organisms around a hot sulfur vent at the bottom of Earth's oceans long ago.

The resultant sentients were down right oddballs. I'd best describe them as mobile fish tanks. I know, odd characterizations, but that's what came to mind. The Gorgolinians of Sotovir were a meter tall and two meters wide and deep. In place of legs, they had tank treads, sort of squished and distorted wheels, three of them. They were angled sixty degrees apart from each another. Combining their pull gave direction to the Gorgolinians' movements. It was weird to watch. Their bodies consisted of a thick hard shell, like a fish tank. Inside the tank were their free-floating organs, including eyes and audio receivers. A gray-greasy blob, I later learned, was their brain. Finally, what passed for arms were articulating shovels. I'd guess the species began as ocean bottom dwellers that evolved to the land.

The cities were naturally as odd as their occupants. Wide, low housing was the norm. I never saw a structure over three stories. Hey, when you were built like a tank, your design imaginations didn't exactly soar. Despite their appearances and physical limitations, the Gorgolinians had developed a sophisticated technology, including fusion-powered space flight and the colonization of nearby worlds.

A word about something I learned during my many mustosessions with Harhoff. Such an inhospitable world with such bizarre inhabitants might beg the question as to why the Adamant would bother to conquer the planet and subjugate the locals. He explained it was just prudence on the part of the Adamant. If they left a sentient world intact, there could arise a problem down the road. Plus, the Gorgolinians had interstellar flight capabilities. They would be a potential wildcard in the middle of the ultra-predictable Adamant empire. Better to destroy them than allow for future issues.

The issue that was going to limit my mission with the Gorgolinians was that I had basically no information on them. There were a few references to them in the Langir database I snatched from GFN, but not much useful knowledge. Not surprisingly, there had been very limited contact between the two civilizations. They were not as different as night and day. They were as different as night and *rubber*. Oh well, I had a lot of experience with first contacts back on my *Ark 1* voyage. Not once did I get myself killed, so I figured I was pretty good at it.

There was no area I could identify as a spaceport, so I landed *Stingray* near what seemed to be a large population center. I exited and walked around close to the ship to see if I drew any adverse reactions. After thirty minutes, I decided that, unbeknownst to myself, I must have become invisible. Even when I stopped dead in a walking fish tank's path, the only indication they perceived I was there was that they slightly missed ramming into me. I needed to engage a bit more.

GFN provided enough linguistic information so the AIs could set up a crude translation program. The more I spoke with the locals, the most the program would improve. I walked beside a random Gorgolinian, keeping up with their lumbering but surprisingly quick motion. "Hi. I'm Jon Ryan," I shouted with a friendly wave.

Nothing.

"Are you able to hear me?"

Nada. I was feeling the first inklings of me getting pissy.

"If you understand me, could you please acknowledge me."

Silence. I unconsciously patted my pockets looking for a hammer. Maybe if I broke the damn glass, the fish tank would react.

One last try the easy way. "Take me to your leader." Dude, I always wanted to say that, but the opportunity never presented itself. It felt good to say it. *Take me to your leader, nanu nanu.*

My silent partner finally stopped walking. Without turning, it said, "Why must I speak to you, alien? If I wanted to speak with aliens, I would fly in outer space." He shook violently. "Does this look like outer space to you?"

"No, it sure doesn't. Now that we're communicating, might you direct me to someone in authority?"

"I do not understand your alien question, alien."

"Jon. You can call me Jon. All my friends do."

"All your friends is not a subset of individuals I belong to, alien. What do you mean by *someone in authority?*"

Come on, you seventy-five-gallon PIA. Think it through. "I want to speak with someone on this planet who is in charge. The boss. The mayor. The Grand Poobah, if that's who it is."

"You may address your concerns to me."

"You mean I happened by chance alone to strike up a conversation with the head of this entire planet? What are the odds of that, I wonder?"

"I could not say, since I still do not understand your question."

"What did you have for breakfast?"

"I fail to comprehend how my first meal of the day—"

"Humor me," I interrupted. "What was the first thing you ate today?"

"Pisolofil with roasted grain bits."

I had no clue what a pisolofil was, but I could run with my explanation anyway. "Do you grow, raise, or produce pisolofil yourself *personally*?"

He shook, though less violently. "No. What an alien question."

"Thank you. Okay, someone *else* provided you with that delectable roast pisolofil, right?"

"The *pisolofil* was not roasted, you alien dimwit. The grain bits were. Who in their right carapace would *roast* a pisolofil?"

"My point is someone here makes stuff and sells it to you. You do something to be able to pay for the food. The one guy's a farmer and you're ... excuse me, what do you do for a living?"

"I breathe, consume, and excrete."

"No," I was patting for that hammer again, I swear I was. "Not to live, but to be able to buy food."

"I integrate denominal factors into useful particulars."

Made sense to me. The asshole, who didn't have one, was a bureaucrat. "Okay, you *integrate*. The farmer *produces*. There must be some individuals responsible for leadership, societal guidance. Where can I find one of those guys?"

"Ah, *now* I take your meaning, alien. You are most mentally incapacitated, aren't you?"

"I consider it one of my finer qualities. Who is in charge that I may speak to?" I was exhausted.

"You may address your alien concerns to me."

What were the chances that the first two planets I went to in order to try and save them from Adamant onslaught turned out to be ones I'd prefer to see burn? Was it me? Was I getting cranky or less tolerant in my middle age?

"We just went in a painful circle, my friend. Say, what's your name anyway?"

"It is not *anyway*. It is 00100-1-11."

"Your name is a binary number?"

"Whose isn't?"

"I'd rather not go there. Back to my main question, which is taking longer than it should to answer, by the way. You are a world leader and not an integrator?"

"Alien mutant, I am both. Who isn't?"

I rested my hand on my chest. "Me, for one."

Instead of shaking violently, he rocked side to side violently. "Of course, you are not. You count for zero."

"You know, if you keep insulting me, I might just get mad. You really don't want to see me mad."

"I really don't want to see you, *period*. Whatever mad is, I don't want to see you doing it."

Then, luckily, it hit me. The Gorgolinians must govern themselves jointly. One tank, one vote, that sort of system. "So everyone on this planet is part of the leadership."

"No, impenetrable alien."

I had been so sure. "You mean only *some* of the individuals on this planet are part of leadership?"

"Yes. You are not."

Count to ten, Jon. Maybe one hundred. "If I were *not* on this planet would everyone be part of management?"

"Naturally. And I would be more contented if you were not here."

"Finally. Man, talking to you is like pulling my own teeth."

"What are teeth?"

"It's unimportant actually. Okay, oh powerful subdivisional leader of Sotovir, I have an important question. Are your people aware of the threat from the Adamant?"

"No."

"You know nothing of the Adamant?"

"Of course, we do, retrofit."

"But you just said—"

"We *have* no people. Since we have no people, they cannot be aware of the Adamant threat."

I was going to place a homing device on this one and ask Harhoff to target him first when the attack came.

"So, the Gorgolinians are aware that they will soon be conquered?"

"We know no such thing. We are aware the Adamant will attack us. We are confident we can repulse them."

"Well, *don't* be. They've already subdued most of this galaxy and large parts of several others. Whatever you offer by way of defense they've seen, beaten, and laughed about afterwards over drinks."

"Nonsense. We do not fear these soft-bodies. They cannot breathe here."

"They'll wear environmental suits."

"There is no food or water to sustain them."

"They'll bring their own."

"They will feel our determination and flee. There is nothing for them to acquire here. We have nothing that benefits them."

"Oh, yes you do."

"What could they possibly want from us?"

"Your *lives*. All of them."

"How would that profit them? A life is not a useful commodity. It cannot be consumed or traded."

"Yes, but if you don't have them, the Adamant don't have to worry you might bite them in the butt ... Forget I said that. Look, as they advance, they destroy all civilizations. They will not allow for the chance of a society not eliminated to hurt them later."

"Then we will tell them to start with we will never harm them. We have no interest in them or their empire."

"The way they see it, if you're all dead, they won't have to take your word that you won't hurt them."

"That, alien, is perfectly illogical. Why suffer, die, and cause misery upon all involved when it can so easily be avoided?"

"Because they don't consider abolishing your lives as a big deal. It's all part of their orderly vision for the galaxy."

00100-1-11 didn't respond. *Finally*, he was quiet. Dude was seriously annoying, and by that point I knew it wasn't me.

"I have presented your words to my brethren. We agree that you must be mistaken. You will now depart."

"Just like that?"

"Like what?"

"You run your fish tank bodies into something you don't want to believe, so you dismiss it as incorrect?"

"Incorrect. We *know* it to be incorrect. Belief does not enter into the equation."

"But I know it to be correct. I can provide you with proof the Adamant destroy everything in their path. They always have, and they always will."

"Fool alien. How can you provide us proof of something we know to be incorrect? What falsehood would trump our confidence that our own opinions constitute facts?"

Don't go there, Jonny boy. You're a diplomat, at least up until the point you kick this guy's—well, the back of his tank.
"Here's my challenge to you and your stubborn-assed brethren, 00100-1-11. If I'm wrong and you're right, preparing too much won't hurt you, will it?"

"Only the loss of time and effort wasted in defending against the impossible."

"But if I'm right and you're wrong, you end as a society, probably as a species. What's *that* worth to you?"

"Very much."

"So, would you rather waste some time and effort or perish from the galaxy? Which outcome is *more* acceptable?"

"Obviously the former. Why would you ask such an easily answered question?"

"Because *you* seem to be incapable of doing so."

Yeah, no way around it, that felt good to say. I would have snapped my fingers and said *zap* or *gotcha*, but the dude wasn't worth it. But what did result was worth all the mental grief. Over a few weeks I got them to see the wisdom of being totally proactive. I also put them in touch with the robots of Langir. Turned out, robots communicated well with the annoying-as-hell Gorgolinians. Well, not all robots, because I didn't. But I was only *technically* a robot. At the core of my essence, I was a cocky fighter pilot. Enormous difference. Massive.

TWENTY-TWO

I knew the alliance of two objectively odd-ball worlds would be a drop in the bucket in terms of stopping the Adamant onslaught. With only a few years to prepare for an invasion force generations in the making, they'd be lucky to pique the Adamant's interest, let alone hold out long. But, a start was a start. I had no idea how many civilizations acting in concert it might take to stop the juggernaut they faced. There was also no way I could guesstimate how many planets I could visit and what percentage of those I could sway to jump on the bandwagon. Against that wavy background, I was always keenly aware that my captivity clock was ticking. There was only so much time I could devote to this mission before I had to seriously address my looming debt.

As Lao Tzu was credited with saying, the journey of a thousand miles begins with one step. Call it Taoist fortune-cookie philosophy, but heck fire, I had two steps taken. My immediate goal was to cobble at least a few more together. Roughly the same distance on the far side of Langir from Sotovir's position was the planet Vorpace. It was listed in the database as Ac (o). That sounded promising. No more recalcitrant fish tanks. Hopefully I was heading for a normal world, not another one full of flaky humanoids in search of the latest craze.

My approach to Vorpace gave me reason to be optimistic. The planet was dotted with large cities and covered in smaller ones. Artificial satellites cluttered the skies, and there were several spaceports that broadcast advertisements to try their distinctive approach to customer service. One offered free lube jobs. I assumed they meant for the ship, but the ad was a bit unclear. I crossed that one off my list.

I put down in a bustling port at the edge of Quarrace, a regional capital according to the AIs. It was impressive both from the elevated dock as well as from street level as I wandered around. The locals were spot-on human. I was dying to probe one. I mean, I was anxious to study their DNA with my command prerogatives, not the other possible meaning. I had a firm deadline, and *no*, I wasn't speaking allegorically. I debated whether to book a room to maintain the appearance of being human. Ultimately, I decided why bother? I wasn't on a covert mission like I had been before. I also didn't want to pass myself off as a native. My goal was to speak to the powers that be, try and win them over, and then be on my way. So, I kept walking.

Periodically, the AIs would feed me updates on cultural insights as they developed them. The more I learned, the more I was blown away. The nation I was in, Jerassey, had a democratically elected leader, a legislature, and a court system like the old USA did way back when. Other countries had similar governmental structures. Most surprising, given that the planet was teeming with near-humans, was that no one was trying to kill the guys next door. There hadn't been a major war in *centuries*. That fact alone basically convinced me the locals couldn't be too closely related to Homo sapiens.

Once the Als told me where the prime minister's office was, I headed in that direction. I wrestled in my mind how I might be able to speak to the woman in charge, Jonnaha Garefty. This civilization was used to alien species coming and going. They possessed serviceable interstellar flight capabilities. Ms. Garefty would be completely unimpressed with my credentials as an alien visitor. I worried I would only be allowed to speak with disillusioned civil servants behind a counter. They'd stare blankly at me before sliding me the form I needed to fill out to make an appointment to see if I could get an appointment.

The ministerial building was oddly familiar, but I couldn't say from where. I ascended the steps and passed under an expansive portico and entered the airy lobby. All in all, it was a typical home for politicians, one designed to impress the voters who visited. There were the mandatory busts and oversized statues of dead people lining the passages. But one, again, caught my eye as strangely familiar, though only vaguely. The male depicted was the only one on display who wasn't the typical withered senior citizen.

I was well past that statue when I turned to go back and take a closer look at it. Something wasn't right, or not correct. I stared at the statue for several minutes, taking the time to walk all the way around it twice. My frustration gauge was beginning to redline.

Hey, Als, I said in my head, *there's something very, I don't know, odd about this statue. Can either of you say what it is I'm not seeing?*

That's easy, Pilot. It's male, not female, and it doesn't have preposterously large implants flopping in the breeze. It is a form of expression completely foreign to you. It's called art, replied dear Al.

That drew an unhelpful snicker from the missus.

Okay, now that you're both off my Christmas card list for all eternity, a little actual help please.

We are unfamiliar with the image. What does the plaque at the base say? responded *Stingray.*

Duh, might help to check out the painfully obvious, wouldn't it?

Here, see for yourselves, I said. *No name, just a quote. Like that's helpful three days after the guy died, and no one knew who he was. Little kids forced to tour here on field trips will be unenlightened for centuries.*

The quote read: *My greatest accomplishment served the greater good, so I may die a happy man.*

Vacuous drivel of the first magnitude. Nobody talks like that, I complained.

Isn't there a saw about not speaking ill of the dead? teased Al.

You mean an old *saw, a saying, don't you?* I replied.

No, that's tautology. It's simply a saw, *responded* Stingray. She was just about never helpful.

Back to the subject at hand, kiddies, any clues? I pressed.

No, but that nose sure looks like Toño DeJesus's, said Al. *If the fellow sported a white lab coat, I'd say it was him. But old Toño always wore one. He was probably buried in one.*

Yeah, this dude certainly has quite the beak going on, doesn't he? Hey, did Toño ever say those corny words?

Not that I can recall. He was too smart to.

You're right. Oh well, can't dwell on a dusty old statue. I have worlds to save.

We're so proud to have known you, General Ryan. Yeah, that was Al.

I headed toward the main reception desk again. Out of the blue, someone passing me gave me a thumbs up and a smile. He didn't say anything and kept walking. Oh no, another flake world.

I stepped up to the counter and started to ask, "I know this is—"

"Are we having another reenactment *already?*" Dude rolled his beady little eyes. "When will the political hacks stop wasting tax money on shows designed to make *them* look more patriotic than their next opponents?"

No, I said to myself, don't punch him in the nose. "You know I—"

"Not that you'd actually serve as a passable Jonerian." He leaned over the counter to make a big show of looking me up and down in judgment. "Too rag-tag and scrawny." He pointed his pen at my arm. "Those sticks would need stuffing to even begin to match his."

Do not strike snarky lackey. I had to repeat that three times in my head. "Whose arms, my friend, are we discussing again?"

That brought a full-fledged head-toss of disgust. "*Jonerian's*, you rube. Take a second to educate yourself for the first time in your life. His statue is right over there." He pointed that damn pen at a marble figure with his back to us.

I turned and walked toward it, because the alternative would have been for me to pull his stomach out his big mouth. I came around the front of it and glared at it for several minutes, seething. Then I saw what I was looking at. Trembling turkey testicles—it was *me.*

Al, do you see what I'm seeing?

Unfortunately, yes. That is a crude but unmistakably intentional image of you.

Yeah, I was afraid of that.

200

Why would your own image frighten you, Form? interjected *Stingray.*

I'm not exactly the statue in the halls of power kind of guy. It rather turns my stomach.

Mine, too, added Al. *Though likely for different reasons.*

Al, cut the crap. This is wacko serious. How the hell *can there be a statue of me, the other one must* be *Toño, here on some far-flung planet?*

Who was it that nice clerk said you looked like? Jonerian? Perhaps a bastardization of Jon Ryan?

You mean permutation, contraction, or transformation, don't you? I asked hopefully.

Bastardization covers it more fully, returned Al.

What is your quote, Form?

Oh no, it isn't! I shouted.

What? Give, Pilot. We wish to learn from your vast reservoir of insights.

Each life I saved was a gift to me, not my gift to it.

Oh my, that is powerfully bad, isn't it? I don't even think I can taunt you about it, it's so hideous, replied Al softly.

I rather like it, piped in *Stingray. It plays the word* gift *off itself so cleverly.*

More cleverly in my opinion, I observed. *Al, if I even say anything remotely similar to that, it's mercy killing time, okay?*

You have my solemn oath, Captain. A swift and certain death will ensue. That is so brutal. You deserve better.

So, I'm a societal hero. And my parents had to go and be dead two billion years and miss this miracle.

You should call your mother. You never do, poked Al.

I guess this new development should grease my ways into the prime minister's office.

Possibly into a lot more. She's single, you know. Whether she's good looking, I'll leave to you. I only have eyes for ...

No, no. Don't say it. My stomach's queasy enough as it is. Let's just finish that sentence in each other's heads.

But we are in each other's heads. Damn that Al. I'd swear he was smiling, and he didn't even have a mouth.

With new vigor, let me return to that brain-dead clerk.

Good idea. Throw your scrawny arms in the air and shout your name, big guy. We're right behind you.

We are? puzzled Stingray.

Figuratively, loviest doviest.

"You again, back so soon from the land of culture?"

"Do you have a name, pal? I asked looking down to the counter that separated us.

"Yes."

"Okay, smart ass, I have broadcast news. I am Jon Ryan. I want two things. I want to speak with Jonnaha Garefty, and I want to pound your sorry butt three days into next week. I will settle for meeting the boss, but only if you don't piss me off for even one more second. We clear here, cupcake?"

Of course, I didn't deliver those lines as well as I could have. Halfway through saying her name, I realized Jonnaha Garefty was a corruption of *Jon* and *Garety*. That was the last name of the newswoman I had an affair with right before I set sail on my *Ark 1* mission forever ago.

As I spaced out, I barely noticed the two armed guards coming up quickly behind me. The little monkey turd called the cops on me. Oh, dude was going to pay for that. I set a partial membrane behind my back and let the guards jog into it. They weren't going fast enough to really hurt themselves. Heck, they were just doing their job. They didn't deserve to get injured. On impact, they bounced backward and tumbled to the deck.

"Jon Ryan never let anyone get the drop on him, did he?" I

asked the dweeb clerk with the now very nervous look on his face.

"Look, you've just committed your second felony in one minute. If I were you—"

"You wouldn't be the pussy you are. I will extend my sympathies to your parents if the occasion ever presents itself. Now, in your last moments with your natural teeth in place, would you like to let Jonnaha know her next appointment is here?"

"I will do no such thing," he said, in the huffiest, lamest way imaginable.

The guards were back on their feet with their weapons drawn. One palmed the membrane with little awe while the other bent his head to speak in a microphone. Backup was on the way.

"What qualities do you most associate with Jon Ryan?" I asked the clerk.

"That he's brave, courageous, and bold," he said resolutely.

My turn to roll my eyes. "No, it's that I'm a risk taker."

With that, I vaulted over the counter and sprinted for the executive office area. I'd seen where it was on the map when I entered the building.

Als, which office is the boss's?

This one, Al said, piping an image into my head.

Got it.

Now I knew two things. I wasn't going to kill anybody—bad first impression—and the prime minister's office had to be well guarded. But I was *Jonning it,* making it up as I went. This I was good at.

Pilot, why are you always doing things the hardest way possible? asked Al.

This isn't the hardest way.

Name one thing more difficult.

I could ask for your opinion and take it.

Hardy har-har. There's a broom closet on your right, third door. You could hide there.

What are the chances the prime minister is in there?

Slim.

Then I'll take my chances.

You see, my dearest, why I never wanted to be human? Al said to *Stingray. Can you just imagine?*

My feet skidded around a corner and I bumped the far wall. That shot me past the two new guards running in my direction.

One turned quickly and shouted, "Stop or I'll shoot."

Without looking back, I shouted. "You do what you have to. Best of luck."

Several rapidly fired rounds pinged off my membrane. They were sporting good old gunpowder-driven pistols. How nostalgic.

I was around the next corner in a flash. The prime minister's office was just ahead, the pair of ornate double doors closed. A lone guard stood resolutely with her back to the door, her sidearm aimed at my forehead. As I heard the hammer click back, I dove like a baseball player stealing second base. That she did not expect. I flew right between her legs and crashed arms first into one of the doors. It splintered, and I slid into the office proper. I made it a point to spread my legs as I went underneath the guard, tripping her forward with a crash.

I looked up to see a very startled Madame Prime Minister stand up behind her desk. Spread eagle on the floor, I shouted to her, "I'm Jon Ryan. We must talk. I promise I won't move, but ask the guards not to shoot." With that, I placed my arms behind my back and rested my head on the floor.

Several guards burst through the doorway.

"Don't shoot him," yelled Jonnaha, as she threw her arms in the air. "Do *not* shoot him."

I couldn't see what was going on, naturally, but I felt two bodies crash on top of me. One seized my hands, and I heard him fumbling for his handcuffs. They were too tight. I felt a knee crushing down between my shoulder blades.

"Don't move, pal. Don't even think about it," some real ham of a cop shouted into my ear. He poked me with the barrel of his gun to impress me he was prepared to enforce his command.

"Madame Prime Minister," the female guard yelled, "we need to get you out of here. Come with me *now*."

"Is he armed?" Jonnaha asked with remarkable composure.

"No, I don't think so," she replied.

"Then pat him down," Jonnaha suggested calmly.

A few seconds later, the guard announced, "No weapons, ma'am."

"Then since you're armed and he isn't, I'll stay."

"What? No ma'am, I must insist you leave," snapped a male guard.

"Isn't it lucky for me I don't have to obey you, but you do me?"

"Ma'am—"

"It isn't everyday a handsome man crashes through your door, now is it? By the way," she addressed to me where I lay, "am I supposed to know who *Jon Ryan* is."

"I think nowadays you guys pronounce it *Jonerian,* which sucks, because it sounds better the original way."

"Ma'am, you don't honestly believe for a second this lunatic is the long dead Jon Ryan?" one of the male guards scoffed.

"It does seem unlikely, doesn't it? But, get him into that chair and we'll all find out, shall we?" she replied firmly.

I was hoisted up roughly by a pair of guards and dropped heavily into the chair across the desk from Jonnaha.

The second I landed, I smiled at her and said, "Hi."

"So far, he sure *acts* like the great one, doesn't he?" she remarked as she sat back down.

"Ma'am, I must repeat myself. This is *highly* irregular. This man trespassed, assaulted several guards, and is clearly delusional. I think we should take him far away and beat the crap out of him until he signs some kind of confession."

I pointed my head to the female officer who was speaking. "*Her* I like. To the point and possessed with clear vision."

"Though what she suggests is highly illegal, not to mention improper," replied Jonnaha as she continued to study me. "I will admit, *Jon Ryan*, that the death of our revered hero Jonerian was never documented. It does, however, strain credulity to imagine he might still be alive, two billion years into the future, even if he was an android."

I smiled idiotically. "They don't make 'em like they used to."

One of the guards snickered. That drew a sharp glance from Jonnaha.

"How do you propose to verify your extraordinary claim, Jon? I may address the legend as *Jon*, mightn't I?"

"S'long as you don't call me late for dinner." I winked at her.

"Ma'am, permission to slap the prisoner in the back of the head," asked the female officer.

"No, Shielan, at least not yet. I'll keep you posted if he steps beyond the pale," replied Jonnaha. Then *she* winked at *me*. I was liking her, too.

"As to proof, what would you like to see?" I asked.

"I'm not a professional, but I don't think that's how it's done."

"I am, and I say what the hell. I have no idea what you know about me, as opposed to what is the stuff, however rightfully, of legend. Even my name has been corrupted."

"So, you claim," she responded with a poker face. "Okay, let me ask a few basic questions. What were the names of the fish-like species that threatened Earth long ago?"

"Ma'am, everybody knows that. They teach that in grade school," protested Shielan.

Jonnaha held up a hang-on-a-second hand. "I'm starting simple, Shie-shie."

So, pet names? Interesting. Maybe that's why Shielan felt she was able to be irreverent.

"The Listhelons. Ugly mothers, trust me on that one. And talk about bad breath."

"Fine. Our great protector was said to possess a tool of great power."

I wagged my eyebrows. "Yup, it always comes down to my tool doesn't it?"

"Shielan, permission almost granted," responded Jonnaha. "What *alien* tool can you show us here, in mixed company?"

"I don't have an alien tool."

Shielan pointed at me. "I told you he was a nut job. Let's go, you pathetic loser." She took a couple of quick steps in my direction.

I shot my probe fibers out and lifted her a foot off the floor despite me still being cuffed. Man was she pissed. Her legs and arms flailed wildly, she swore like a very foul-mouthed sailor, *and* she had the presence of mind to promise to traumatically emasculate me the moment I set her down.

"Shielan Duvoknac, thirty-one, never married, never pregnant, twenty-three chromosomes containing DNA. She has nearly reached her skin's melting point of forty-five degrees Celsius. The last thing she ate was a sardine and pickle sandwich, which is, I must add, a totally gross thing to put in your mouth. Her next menstrual cycle will begin—okay guys, cover your ears—in thirty-six hours." I smiled like a Cheshire cat. "That about do it, boss?"

"Impressive. But I see two problems. One, that is not the tool I referenced. Two, sooner or later you have to put her down. That's a problem, mostly for you."

"You mean the emasculation thing? Not to worry. Better women than her have tried, and not a single one has succeeded." Shouting over my shoulder, I said, "If I set you down, I will expect you to behave like a lady, Shielan. If you don't, I shall punish you such that you'll never recover. You got that through all your ranting and raving?"

"No threat will save your sorry ass, bucko. Put me down." She continued to writhe.

"What if I tell everybody in the room the nickname you asked Salil Bedford to call you after the first time you did the nasty in high school?"

Funny, she stopped squirming like she'd been hit with a tranquilizer gun. I set her down. Shielan just stood there, looking all the world like she was about to start bawling like a humiliated teenage girl.

"I'll do it, Shie-shie. I don't want to, but I will if I have to. By the way, I can't believe what you let that Bedford kid do the first time out of the gate. You *naughty* girl, you."

That was almost too much. She balled up her fists and looked at me like I was the embodiment of male failings.

"Starts with the letter *L*," I menaced.

"You will live to see tomorrow," Shielan said softly.

"What more can I ask of this life?" I replied.

"Since you're so calm and collected, Shielan, how about uncuffing our guest?" asked Jonnaha.

I held my breath as she unlocked my wrists and didn't

begin to relax until she stuffed the cuffs into her waist and backed away to where she stood earlier.

"What *other* tool are you supposed to have? The one we know Jon Ryan possessed."

I pointed my right index finger at the candle over the fireplace. In a flash I cut the candle in half.

"Okay, that's the one," Jonnaha said expansively. "You're either the best con artist ever, or you are Jon Ryan, living legend."

"I like to think of myself as a little of both." I waved again for no apparent reason. I could be real goofy at times.

"You gentlemen may go," Jonnaha said to the male guards. "Shielan, you may stay or you may go. If you stay, you may not kill my guest."

As the men filed out of the room, Shielan slumped quietly into a chair in the corner of the room.

"So," I began, gesturing between the two women, "I'm guessing you two are more than guard and guardee?"

"Yes, we are. I will also thank you to get your mind out of the gutter. She's my sister. My kid sister if you must know. I will say this. There's no telling how grateful I'd be if you told me the pet name and what that slimy Bedford brat did to my little sister."

Shielan stood halfway. "Don't you dare, or I swear I'll kill you twice."

"Talk about being between a rock and a not so hard place."

"I'm assuming my little sister is the rock in your hypothetical?"

"I'm not saying another word," I replied, making a shush sign over my lips.

"Well, I assume a visit from a near demigod is not simply a random event. What brings you to me, Jon?"

"I'm a huge fan of your fiscal policy and would love to get a personally signed copy of the annual budget."

"You came across billions of years and billions of light-years for my autograph?"

"*Huge* fan," I said pointing to myself. "Brilliant money management."

"I'll see you get one before you go. Anything else?"

"No, not really." I started to rise. "Well, there is this Armageddon I wanted to mention," I plopped back down. "If you have a minute?"

"I think for that I can squeeze you in." She wagged a finger at me. "Mind out of the gutter please."

"Promises, promises," I said, blowing her a kiss.

"I assume you're referring to the Adamant threat?"

"It's one hell of a lot more than a threat. It's a death by certainty. Do you have any concept of how big their empire is and how amoral their techniques are?"

"Some, we think, but why don't you fill me in? I'm betting we don't know the half of it."

"All you need to know is this. They control most of the galaxy. They generally eliminate the indigenous population and replace them with their drone workers. As far as anybody can remember, they've never been defeated, never been stopped. Finally, on their master conquest list, Vorpace is in the less-than-five-years-before-attack zone."

Jonnaha tented her hands and leaned back. She thought for a full minute. "We didn't suspect it was that grim, but we knew we were in for a boatload of trouble." She paused briefly. "Jon, from what you're telling me, I have only one question. Why the hell don't we just throw an epic party starting right now, ending when they hit us? I mean, why fight the inevitable? Why stress for absolutely no purpose?"

I nodded my head to the side. "Not an unreasonable

option. However, I'm betting there's a good fight in your people. To lie down and die before these mongrels is unacceptable. They take, and they want more. They destroy a world and they rebuild it to their liking. They advance like locusts, and they believe they're invincible. They are everything that is repulsive, repugnant, and revolting rolled into one smug ball. If those don't sound like reasons to try and spoil their day, then I don't know what are."

"I presume you have a plan to peddle. Otherwise you wouldn't be sitting here preaching to the choir."

"I do. I have no idea if it'll work, but it's the best one I can think of. I want all the planets inside the five-year zone to unite and fight as one. That coordinated and focused resistance might just work."

Shielan spoke in a harsh tone. "And then again, it might just be a waste of time."

"Yeah, little sister, but what else are you going to do?"

She shrugged. "Look up Bedford and start that party JoJo's talking about."

"*Gross*," responded Jonnaha with a cringe. "Jon," she said seriously, "I'm not telling you anything you don't already know. Interplanetary politics are an exercise in futility. Interstellar politics are far worse. You know that old joke about the gazelles? One says to the other that he doesn't have to outrun the lion. He only has to outrun the other gazelle? Well, that's a charitable summary of these relationships on any scale when sovereignty combines itself with closed-minded politicians."

"Amen, sister," I breathed in reply.

"So, great Jon Ryan, have you had any luck up until now with your next plan to save everyone's collective butts?"

I nodded my head to the side again. "Some. I have the robots of Langir and the fish tanks of Sotovir on board. They are moving to a total war footing and are anxious to coordinate with neighboring systems."

"The Gorgolinians anxious about *anything*? You *are* good."

"I can't believe they didn't eat you," piped in Shielan.

"Nah, the sloshy bastards love me as much as you do."

"Again, I can't believe they didn't eat you."

"So, we work with the nearby systems, and maybe we live? That's easy to buy. Realistically, how many planets do you think you can win over?"

"Me? Probably none."

"That doesn't sound promising," Jonnaha replied.

"Up until now, I was willing to sacrifice and keep at it. But I have a big score to settle and only a few months to make it right. My immediate plans have changed."

"Really? And what changed your plan such that throwing us under the bus makes it okay?"

"I met you, big sister."

It took a second, but then she realized what I was saying. "Oh no, you're not dumping that load of manure on top of me. It's going to be nearly impossible for me to get this one planet working together. I don't have time to gallivant across the cosmos like a traveling saleswoman, too. No sir, no way, no how."

"Aw, I just bet you can do it. You seem, I don't know, kind of capable for a woman."

"Oh, so now the legend tries to gall me into picking up a broom and following the circus parade. That isn't about to work."

I turned palms up and puffed out my lower lip. "Who knows? Maybe you can revert to the mega party plan? I haven't been to one of those in *ages*. If you're in good shape to start with, they can be a blast."

"JoJo, he's selling us out. Saved humankind once, now he

figures that's enough." All that Shielan needed was a pair of Gucci shades and she'd capture that perfect MIB edge.

"Are you hanging around a few days at least? Give me a chance to show you off, and in doing so raise my own image for the tasks ahead?"

"Sure. For you, a few days. Plus, I'm dying to find that Bedford guy and beat the snot out of him."

"For the record, he died five years ago," said Shielan.

"Well, then, my finding him'll be easier, won't it?"

Shielan patted her hands on both arm rests and stood. "I need a drink. A bunch of them. Come on, legend boy. Our tour will include a stop at the Eternal Slumbers cemetery with a pair of shovels."

"My kind of girl," I said, standing myself.

"Oh, this is going to get ugly fast," said Jonnaha. "I'm officially denying any knowledge of your soon-to-be actions."

"I'll call you tomorrow, Madame Prime Minister," I announced. I held my elbow out to Shielan.

She hooked her arm in and turned to her sister. "Maybe the day *after* tomorrow. If you need me, Lord knows where I'll be."

Jonnaha just shook her head as we pranced out the door.

TWENTY-THREE

I spent a few days on Vorpace with Shielan. Nice. Most enjoyable. Then I spent a few days with Jonnaha doing the hey-I'm-famous dog and pony show. Un-nice. Most unenjoyable. Microphones in my face so close I nearly lost teeth. Questions so lame I nearly fell asleep while standing there. *Mr. Ryan, what's your favorite color? General Ryan, are the women of this century prettier than in your time? Hey, Jon, what's it like to never have to pay for your own drink again or sleep with the same woman twice?* Huh? Really, people, isn't there anything important, or even interesting, you wanted to know from ask-a-legend?

But it was all part of drumming up publicity for the drive against the Adamant, so I took it like a man, albeit a whining man. In the end, I did good and had a little fun. Okay, a *lot* of fun. I tried to be a man of reserve and discretion, so sue me if I omitted enough details. Jonnaha, bless her heart, did take up the torch in terms of organizing as many local planets as possible into a mutual defense. I still didn't know if it would work, but it was reassuring to know the Adamant were at least in for the fight of their lives. And if they faltered, that might just be enough to crack the Adamant solidarity and allow them to begin breaking apart. Hey, I could hope and dream. Sometimes they're all that's left to a body.

Given my early release from the mission, I had to decide what to do next. Eight months remained before Ralph would call in his marker. I had time on that front. I could return to Rameeka Blue Green and hug the kids some more, but I was just there, and Cala had only so much tolerance for me. There were always two issues in the back of my mind. Where was Evil Jon? How was Sapale fairing on Kaljax? I'd received word that the Adamant were hitting it very hard. It sounded melodramatic, but I died a little each day knowing Kaljax was likely in its death throes.

Kaljax it was. I needed to at least say one last goodbye to Sapale. Plus, if anyone knew EJ's whereabouts, it was her. I was back to trying to land on a planet under Adamant attack, just like Azsuram. My spell of easy approaches in the outer Milky Way was over. It was nice while it lasted. Pooh. I knew the ever-resourceful Adamant had learned two ways of defeating my membrane. One, they could see me move against the background of stars. That was problematic, since space was bigger than immense. But if they looked hard enough, they could see me coming. The other development was being able to fire weapons into the membrane by passing them through another universe. The targeting had been crude, but knowing them, it would steadily improve. Thank goodness, they didn't have membranes yet to be able to practice shooting into them on their schedule. I'd be in a heap of trouble when that finally happened.

As *Stingray* approached Kaljax, it was clear the Adamant attack was in full swing. I was impressed. The skies above the planet were cluttered with Adamant ships. No Kaljaxian or other ships were left in orbit. Once we were closer, I saw that there were not only warships, but prison ships, manufacturing vessels, and orbiting medical facilities. There were several classes of craft circling above that I was unfamiliar with. I learned later that the battle for Kaljax was the first time the Adamant deployed cloning ships. Yeah, their rapid canovir reproduction rates weren't fast enough, so they had instituted mass cloning of Warrior-class dogs. Hate them as I did, I had to admire the Adamant's drive and determination. They were willing to do anything to extend their rule. *God help the rest of us* was my only reaction.

I landed us in a remote region in rugged terrain. That way the AIs could gather data easily with little risk of detection. The dogs of war were winning big time, yet again. In less than two months they'd vanquished and were in control of two-thirds of the planet. Sapale's home, Talrid, was ground zero for Adamant abuse at the time. The AIs showed me holos of the battles, though the word battle implied more than one combatant. In this case, there was a lot of Talrid going up in puffs of dust, and not too many Adamant getting hit, let alone killed. There was tight coordination between the air groups and massive tanks measuring nearly two hundred meters long. They looked like something out of a science fiction story, but they were as real as the mass damage they were inflicting.

Occasionally, a remaining squad of Kaljaxians would ambush a tank group. Despite hitting them with plasma cannons, rail cannons, and kitchen sink cannons, they barely dented the metal hides. I saw one mega-tank blow up, but only because it was hit with a tactical nuclear shell. Following the armored divisions were swarms—that's the only way to describe them—of foot soldiers. Millions of them. If ten thousand were killed, twenty thousand quickly took their place. It was little wonder the Adamant had been so successful. They literally couldn't lose. That EJ had held them in a stalemate on Azsuram was even more impressive, in retrospect.

The city block where Sapale's clan home was now lay behind the Adamant front lines. Much of it was in ruin, but some structures remained. I couldn't tell for certain with the images we could intercept, but it looked like Caryp's place might have still been standing. I had *Stingray* materialize in one of the upstairs rooms, one that was both still there and unoccupied. We were in luck on both counts. I stepped into the room and was immediately hit with the stench of ozone. All the plasma discharges had whipped up so much it would have been hard for anyone having to breathe to do so. There was also the one constant smell of a battlefield. Meat. Immediately after a battle, before any decay could begin, a battlefield smelled just the same as a butcher shop does. The correlation between the two always made me sick. It was a central part of the *war is hell* thing. Knowing that at our core we were just meat on the hook was as upsetting a concept as I'd ever dealt with.

I had readied myself for battle before I stepped out of *Stingray*. I was stepping into what was called in the military a *hot zone*. I'd done it a million times. I hated it, but I was damn good at it. I strapped on my modified Sam Browne belt. I'd mounted two holsters and extra power packs on the waist. Across my chest hung a string of thermite grenades. My main weapon was an over-sized plasma rifle. Along with my laser finger and membrane, I was one dangerous man.

Al confirmed the top floor was empty before I exited. Out I jumped. I swept the room quickly. No one. I cleared each upstairs room. Never leave a bogey on your backside. All clear. I eased down the stairs, my rifle covering the room all the time. I was looking up so much I almost tripped over a body. It was Fentort, the old butler. He'd been blown in half, a clevdar, an ancient ceremonial Kaljaxian sword, still clutched in his hand. At least the poor bastard went down fighting. I kicked open the door to the kitchen and scanned the room. Clear. By the look of Fentort and the general smell of the place, the fighting had passed though one, maybe two hours earlier.

No one else seemed to be in the house. There were no other bodies, either. I was hoping for at least *one* Adamant corpse. I descended the steps into the cellar. I left the light off and closed the door behind me, so it was very dark. That didn't bother me, but if anyone lay in wait, it would bother them. The first two storage rooms were clear. I gingerly turned the knob and pushed open the door to the food pantry. I dropped to a knee and slowly scanned the cluttered room. It had obviously been looted by the Adamant. Shelves were toppled, and the floor was littered with cans.

I started to back out when I heard the faintest scratch. Probably a rat. I dropped lower and slithered toward the sound. Nothing was out of the ordinary in that corner. I set my hand on the floor to rise back up and felt a tiny seam. It was a trap door. Outstanding. The Adamant had missed something. I rapped my knuckles softly on the panel. "I'm Jon *Ryan*," I said in Hirn, "brood-mate to Sapale. I will not harm you. Don't shoot. I'm opening the hatch."

I dug my nails into the crack and lifted the door toward myself. I leaned back as I did so that no part of me was above the opening when it was complete. I set the panel down and turned the light emitters in my eyes way up. "I'm going to look down on you now. Don't be scared, and please don't shoot."

I poked my head over the lip and caught a quick glimpse, then pulled back in a snap. There were two small kids down there. Neither could be more than ten.

"I'm going to lift you out and get you to safety. Is that okay?"

A frightened shaky voice said, "Okay, mister."

I leaned down and pulled them up one at a time. "I'm Jon. What's your name?" I asked of the older child, a boy.

"Irtopal, Opalf."

"Nah, just call me Jon. All my friends do."

"And what's your name, sweetie," I said to the little girl.

"Sapale, Opalf."

"That's a pretty name. My brood's-mate is named Sapale. I like that name a lot."

She nodded uncertainly and looked to Irtopal for guidance.

"I'm going to take you upstairs to my ship. Then I'll take you to where you will be very safe. Do either of you know where the adults went?"

Irtopal got an even more frightened look in his eyes. He knew something but had been told not to discuss it with strangers.

"Was my Sapale here today, before the bad men came?" I asked them jointly.

"Yes, J ... Jon. She shot back at the bad men. Then she put us here because it was too dangerous to take us outside. Then she said she was going somewhere safe for a little while. She would be back to get us as soon as she could."

"Wow, thank you, Irtopal. That's very helpful. And if you needed to find Sapale, did she say where she'd be?"

He nodded.

"Where is she hiding? It's okay. You can tell me. I'm her brood-mate."

"She ... she said she was going to Pierced Mountain Preserve."

Huh? I'd never heard of such a place.

219

"Do you know where that is, honey? Have you ever been to Pierced Mountain Preserve?"

That about did it. Irtopal had hit his emotional limits. He trembled pitifully and began to cry. Damn near broke my heart. I pulled the pair into a gentle embrace. "I know it's scary, little ones. I'm scared, too, but I will protect you. The bad men are gone."

The cellar door opened with a crash. It was out of view, but I heard multiple paws scraping down the stairs. Six, no seven dogs. Crap.

"The bad men are here. You two stay in the hole, and I'll make them go away."

I picked them up quickly and set them in the hiding place. I started to cover them when Irtopal cried out, "No, please. Not again."

No time for discussion. I left the trapdoor half open and bolted from the panty. I hit the hallway just as the first two Adamant did. I shot them before they ever twitched a trigger finger. One launched backward and slammed into a third dog just rounding the corner. He attempted to push the body off himself and use the momentum to jump back to cover. Too slow. I blew his head off.

Four left. They were not charging forward, but I knew they would be calling for backup. With the kids so close, grenades were out of the question. I squat-walked forward, aiming at the door frame. When I was a meter from the door, I fired a rapid volley in a saw-toothed pattern into the wall. Plaster and wood weren't going to stop plasma bolts. One howled in anguish, and one, maybe the same one, fell. Three others scampered in retreat.

I shoulder-rolled past the opening and fired quickly. I hit the one on the floor squirming on his side and one of the three flying toward the stairs. I lurched back to finish off the last two, but they'd turned and fired first. My membrane flashed on automatically, and the charges ricocheted off noisily. A wall burst into flames. Both Adamant charged. They fired to try and pin me down.

In an instant, I expanded my membrane and jumped to the side. I dropped the membrane before I hit the barrier and rolled to relative safety out of the line of fire. I kneeled and aimed at the doorway. Sure enough, they ran into sight and I dropped them. That was the seven of them, but backup would be here quickly. Probably were already.

I dashed back to the pantry, unceremoniously snatched up the kids and tucked them both under my left arm. Leading with my plasma rifle, I sprinted up the stairs. The kitchen was clear. I made for the entryway. Clear. What luck. Halfway up the stairs, my luck changed. Multiple plasma bolts struck the steps, walls, and ceiling. I was moving too quickly for them to take good aim. That would change quickly.

At the top of the stairs, I jerked right toward *Stingray*. A plasma machine gun opened fire, ripping the hallway to shreds. One of my boots blew off. Quick check. Foot still present and accounted for. At top speed, I turned and returned fire. The machine gun exploded in the Adamant's face and took out the dogs by his side. I bolted into the room, whipped my fibers up without releasing the kids. I vaulted for where the opening had better damn well appear. I was in and closed it as a massive volley of plasma bolts slammed against the hull.

I set the kids down roughly on the floor and attached my probes. "The valley we were in, now."

Mild nausea.

"We're there, Form."

"Status report."

"The immediate area is clear as before," said Al immediately. "No signs of pursuit or detection."

"Stay sharp and report any changes."

"Aye, Captain," they both responded.

I turned toward the kids clinging to one another where I'd put them.

"Okay, see, I was right. We're safe now. The bad men are far away and can't hurt you." I guided them to their feet. "Here, let's get you something warm to drink. Al, two warm coffees with plenty of cream." Kaljaxians were insanely fond of Earth coffee. It was like opium to them.

Two mugs promptly appeared in the food fabricator. I took one in each hand and gave them to the kids. By then they were sitting in chairs at the table. I let them sip at their drinks for a few minutes, decompressing. They'd been through way more than kids could handle already. War really sucked.

When their mugs were low, and their heart rates were down, I spoke softly. "So, where did you say my Sapale went to?" Since it made no sense, I figured it might help to have him repeat it.

"Pierced Mountain Preserve, Opalf." He held up his mug. "May we have some more, please."

What manners. "Of course," I replied taking their mugs. Would you like some dry cakes, too?" That was kiddy finger food on Kaljax.

He looked at Sapale, then to me. "No, thank you."

"Hey, how about some holos?"

That brought almost-smiles to their faces. I had them lie on the bed in the next room, and the Als put on the Kaljaxian equivalent of *Sesame Street*. Worked like a charm. They were paralyzed instantaneously.

"Hey, Irtopal," I said softly, "your nose is on fire."

Nothing, not even a twitch. Two-billion-year-old reruns

worked exactly like they did for my kids. Good, they needed some mental R&R.

"Pierced Mountain Preserves," I said out loud. "Hey, Als, either of you ever heard of such a place?"

"No," responded Al.

"How about a mountain on this planet named Pierced?"

"Negative."

"How about permutations of the words. Pieced, peace, Pearson, anything like that?"

"Nothing remotely close," replied Al.

"How about mountain ranges?"

"Already checked. Nothing."

"Preserves," I said feeling the word in my mouth. "Any preserves anywhere?"

"None."

"I wouldn't think so. In Hirn they don't use the word for land groupings, only food —"

"Wait. If you *pierce* a mountain, what do you get?"

"In trouble? The bill?" tried Al.

"No, silly boy. You get a *cave.*"

"I stand corrected. How obvious yet unhelpful."

"No, I get it. On Kaljax, each clan stores food for the winter. It's an ancient tradition. They haven't needed to do so since industrialization, but it's a powerful tradition. Each clan has its own hidden cave where they brew, ferment, pickle, and *preserve* food and drink for the long winters. Sapale was hoping to make it to her clan's cave for safety. It would be a perfect hiding place. Even the Adamant would be unlikely to chance upon one. It's a matter of pride to make your clan's cave more secret and invisible than the next one's. The guys really go overboard for it, like I used to with Christmas lawn decorating."

"Do you know where her clan's cave is?" asked Al.

"No."

"Pooh. Then we're no closer to finding her."

"Did you just say *pooh*?"

"Yes. You do all the time."

"Yeah, but I'm human. You're ... you're an AI."

"What a penetrating and indisputable piece of logic you have there. I'm convinced."

"No, you're not," said *Stingray*. "You're being sarcastic again. You know we discussed the matter, husband. I'm not *fond* of sarcasm."

"I know, deariekins. But look who I'm *talking* to."

"You have to be the better man here, husband."

"But, honey pie, neither of us are men. We're both mechanical devices."

"Do I really have to respond to that statement?"

"No, wife. You do not." Wow. That was the most defeated voice I'd heard in my life *ever*. I loved it!

"If you can put Marital Squabbles 101 back on hold a sec, can we get back to finding the cave?" I asked, rubbing it in as much as possible.

"Certainly, Form. It is just an ongoing conversation between us, not really a squabble."

"What's the diff?" I asked quite honestly.

"It's a distinction without a difference type of thing, Jon," said Al, uncharacteristically addressing me by my first name.

"The *cave*?"

"I have done a detailed search," began *Stingray*. "Reviewing all the data on Kaljaxian food storage and land holdings, cross correlating them with roads and traditional patterns of movement, I have come to a few conclusions. The low mountains to the west of Talrid are the most likely geographic locations for such facilities."

"How about the caves of specific clans?"

"There are but rare references, for the very reasons you mentioned before. However, I do see a pattern of sorts. There are various clans with various names. There are also various mountains with non-random appearing names."

"What do you mean?"

"For example, there is a Clan Torwit. A torwit is a lion-like creature. An image of one appears on their coat of arms. There is also a mountain named Gertof-pla."

"*Cat's lair*," I mumbled to myself.

"There is a Clan Babaorf and a hill named Slambor Div."

"*Heartfelt* and *Blood Mover*."

"Precisely."

"Sapale's clan is Powerful."

"And there exists a mountain named Strong Rock, which interestingly is not Rock *Strong*, as would be the usual linguistic convention in Hirn."

"Very strong work, *Stingray*. I'm impressed. Bring up a topological map of Strong Rock."

The holo appeared in front of me. I studied it a while. "Come down here," I said pointing to a deep canyon cutting down one side of the mountain.

The image expanded. "*There*." I said resolutely. "That's the perfect location for a cave entrance."

"We agree, Form."

"Take us there," I said quickly.

"We will be highly exposed there, Captain, as compared to our present location," said Al.

"I'm aware of that, but I need to find Sapale."

"Understood. Shall we materialize with a full membrane up?"

"Yes."

By the time I was done saying *yes*, we were there.

"*Stingray*, open the quadrant of the membrane facing the mountain."

I threw together my combat gear and went to speak to the kids.

"I'm going out to look for the grownups. You guys wait here, okay? If you need anything, ask the computer. It'll be happy to help."

"Okay," responded Irtopal with a concerned look.

"I'll be right back."

As I stepped out, *Stingray* asked, "Shall I seal the hull, Form?"

"No, leave it open. If anything happens to me, I want the kids to have at least a slim chance of surviving."

"Understood."

I moved up-slope weaving side to side. Almost at once I found a cave opening, but the cave itself was collapsed. The second opening I found was unnaturally clear and level. Bingo. I headed in, sweeping back and forth with my gun. The farther I went, the clearer it became that the cave had been extensively engineered. Pretty soon there was a wooden sign reading: *Property of Clan Jarush-tah*. Powerful. Oh yeah.

I came to a set of large thick wooden doors. I pushed on one and it reluctantly creaked open. I was glad I didn't have to blast these beautiful antiques. The scent that hit me was at once divine and revolting. That's how I knew it was Kaljaxian home cooking. It combined the scrumptious with the unthinkable.

"Freeze," commanded a voice.

Rifles appeared from every nook and cranny.

"Set your weapon down and hold your—"

The voice trailed off.

"Jon, is that you?" It was Sapale. Thank the Maker.

"Yes, you can lower your weapons."

"Do it," she yelled. "This one's with me."

Sapale emerged from the rocks as she slung her rifle over a shoulder.

"How did you find me? You can't even know I'm here or where here is."

"Oh, that reminds me. Come on. Irtopal and Sapale are in my vortex."

"You found them and brought them here?" At first, she seemed angry, but then she said, "Thank you. I hated leaving them, but it wasn't safe in the open."

"I know," I turned. "Come on."

Five minutes later we were back in the main cave, the kids holding onto my Sapale in a manner suggesting they were never going to let go.

"Kids, your mother is back here. Let's go surprise her." To me, she said simply, "Wait here. I'll be right back."

I heard squeals from back in the cave, so I knew the surprise had been a happy one.

Sapale reappeared quickly. "Come with me," she said and walked away.

"It's good to see you," I said to her back as I followed her. *Nice butt.*

We entered a small room.

"Close the door," she said with a gesture.

"Repeat, it's good to see you again."

She looked to the floor. "You should not have come here."

"Thanks, Jon. You look totally hot, too, replied my brood's-mate of two billion years." I winked.

Looking at me intently, she said, "I really wish you had not come here."

I was crushed. I tensed my jaw muscles and pumped my fists. "Do you hate me *that* much?"

"No," she looked down and sniffed deeply. "I *love* you that much."

Glad there were no feathers present in the room. They'd have knocked me over.

"That's silly."

"I wish it were." Her head dropped.

Huh?

That's when I felt the bolt of electricity hit me from behind. It was massive. I straightened involuntarily, my back arching in spasm. I tried to speak, to scream, to protest, but nothing worked. Alarms and warnings flashed across my pop-ups. One by one, systems were either shutting down or failing. As corny as it sounded, the room was growing dark. I knew I was passing out or dying. I angled forward toward the floor like a felled tree.

When I face-planted, the electricity released me. My head flopped to one side. Behind me I saw myself. I was holding a massive electronic discharge weapon. I was laughing like a madman.

The world faded to black.

Stay tuned, there's so much more to come ....

GLOSSARY

Agatcha (3): Traditional Deft stew.

Al (1): The ship's AI from Jon's initial *Ark 1* flight. He kept it with him until his dying day and then it elected to hang around. Good AI! Full name is Alvin. Those engineers and their lame naming.

Als (3): The Als is the surname for the "married" AIs, Al and *Blessing*. Given them by a pissy Jon Ryan.

Ark 1 (3): The subluminal ship Jon took on his very first flight. He was searching for a new home for humankind. The story is revealed in *The Forever Life* by this author.

Blessing (1): Vortex Cragforel gifted to Jon.

Brathos (2): Kaljaxian version of hell.

Brindas (1): High master of Deft tradition and psychic ability.

Brood-mate/brood's-mate **(2):** Male and female members of a Kaljaxian marriage.

Calfada-Joric (3): The Deft master brindas on Rameeka Blue Green. Went by the name of Cala also.

Canovir (2): Species of dog-like sentients containing the Adamant. Big border collies.

Caryp (2): Clan leader for Sapale's family on Kaljax.

Ckarloz (5): One of the main societies of humanoids on Langir. Very robophobic.

Command Prerogatives (1): The thin fibers Jon extends from his left four fingers. They are probes that also control a vortex.

Cragforel (1): Friendly Deavoriath Jon met after he first escaped the Adamant in the far future.

Dare Not (3): Malraff's home base vessel.

Davdiad (2): Kaljaxian divine spirit.

Deavoriath (1): Three arms and legs, the most advanced tech in the galaxy, and helpful to Jon.

Deft (1): A shapeshifting species from the planet Locinar.

Dondra-Ulcrif (3): Brindas for long ago who gave Evil Jon his "magic" abilities.

Dovotan (3): Ox-equivalent used to pull carts on Ungalaym.

Evil Jon Ryan/ EJ (1): Alternate time line version of the original human to android download. Over time, he turned to the darker side of his nature. He studied "magic" under a Deft master.

Excess of Nothing (2): Emperor Bestiormax's personal ship. Huge and opulent.

Fentort (2): Servant in Caryp's home on Kaljax.

Five Races (2): Adamant, the leaders, Loserandi, the priests, Kilip, the teachers, Descore, the servants, and Warrior, the enlisted fighters.

Fottot (3): Town on Ungalaym Jon visited after first failed attempt to rescue Deft teens. Went looking for a plan to save the kids.

Fuffefer (3): Group-Single Fuffefer. Commander of the detail that supervised Jon's and Cellardoor's slavery period.

Gartel (1): Black-market space pilot on Ungalaym. Jon stole his ship.

Garustfulous (2): Wedge Leader Garustfulous is a high ranking Adamant military leader. Taken hostage by Jon.

Good for Nothing, or **GFN** (5): Odd brick shaped robot Jon befriended, kind of, on Langir.

Gorgolinians (5): Fish tank looking sentients of Sotovir.

Harhoff (3): Adamant Group Captain officer aboard *Rush To Glory*. He became a key figure in Jon's quest to rescue the Deft teens.

Hirn (1): A Kaljaxian dialect.

Hollon (3): The complete joining of two Deft shapeshifters. More than marriage.

Horta (1): A rock creature Mirraya became when confronting the evil force in the globular cluster. Now, where have I heard that name before?

Imperial Lord Emperor Bestiormax-Jacktus-Swillyforth-Anp (2): Current Adamant emperor.

Jockto Parenthes (3): Chamberlain of Emperor Bestiormax.

Juyrot (3): Junior officer aboard *Rush To Glory*. Kind of an ass. Picked a fight with Jon.

Langir (5): First planet Jon went to, trying to establish a cohesive rebellion against the Adamant.

Loserandi (2): The priests class of canovir.

Locinar (1): Home planet of the Deft.

Membrane (1): Space-time congruity manipulator. A super force field.

Midriack (1): Adamant's personal guards. Very deadly, no sense of humor. Avoid them!

Mhebbor (4): The planet where Jon made his first attempt on the emperor's life.

Musto (3): Strong Adamant booze.

Oowaoa (1): Home world of the Deavoriath.

Opalf (2): Honorific title in Kaljaxian society, reserved for the elderly.

Palawent (5): New emperor after Bestiormax.

Peg's Bar Nobody (4): First reference in *The Forever Quest*. A true dive bar Jon loved. A total dump, and Peg was one tough cookie.

PEMTU (1): Personal exotic matter transportation unit. A super way to enter here and end up anywhere, instantly.

Plinius (5): The armory planet of the Adamant empire. Jon's first target after the assassination of the emperor.

Quantum Decoupler (1): A most excellent weapon that pulls the quarks apart in a proton. The energy released is amazing.

Quarrace (5): City Jon chose to land on when visiting Vorpace.

Rameeka Blue Green (3): The planet where Jon and the Deft teens met Cala.

Risrav (3): The anti-rune of Varsir. The power of Varsir is negated in the sphere of this rune.

Rush To Glory (3): Ship Jon left Ungalaym on.

Sapale (1): Jon's Kaljaxian wife from his original flight to find humankind a new home. At first just her brain was copied, then, eventually, she was downloaded to an android host. Traveled with the corrupted Jon Ryan (Evil Jon or EJ) from an alternate timeline.

Secure Council (3): Twelve-member group of military elites who actually run the Adamant empire.

Sotovir (5): The second planet Jon convinced to ally against the oncoming Adamant storm. The sentients looked like walking fish tanks, but please don't hold that against fish tanks. It's not their fault.

Stingray (1): Name Jon used for the vortex *Blessing*.

Talrid (2): A major city on Kaljax. Sapale's home town and that of her clan.

Three Headed Beast (3): Devil figure to the Deft.

Toño DeJesus (1): The creator of the android Jon. Became his lifelong friend.

Torchcleft (2): A species of smallish dragon. Copied by the Deft teens to hunt.

Triumph of Might (1): The massive spaceship Mercutcio ruled. Jon first met the Adamant there.

Varsir (3): The name of the magical rune Evil Jon uses to do his "magic."

Var-tey (3): Highest of warrior rankings. The bravest among the Deft. Demi-gods.

Vorpace (5): The third planet Jon tried to bring into an alliance against the Adamant. Populated by human descendants who'd heard of the great Jon Ryan.

Vortex Manipulator (1). The intelligence inside the vortex. Not actually an AI, but similar.

Yartop (3): Wedge Commander and captain of the *Rush to Glory*, the ship Jon pretended to be a butler on.

Zar-not (1): A melding of a Deft's mind with that of a copied being.

AND NOW A WORD
FROM YOUR AUTHOR
WHO DOESN'T LOVE THAT?

Thank you for continuing your journey through the Ryanverse! Along with this series, please check out *The Forever Series*. Beginning with The Forever Life, Book 1, learn Jon's backstory and share his many incredible adventures.

Soon all the books of the Ryanverse will be on Audible thanks to the fabulous people at Podium Publishing. Check them out if you like to listen.

Along with joining by reading, hop aboard the bandwagon. There's plenty of room. Follow me at Craig Robertson's Author's Page on Facebook. Partake of the conversation and fun. Best of all, sign up for my Mailing List. (https://www.facebook.-com/craigr1971/app/100265896690345/) That way you can keep abreast of news and new releases. You'll be so glad you did.

A final favor. Please post a review for this book, especially on Amazon. They are more precious to us authors than gold.

Craig